24 Carrot Caper

Marcall's Breakfast Cafe Paranormal Cozy Mystery

B I Skinner

Contents

Chapter 1

"Good morning, Gladys!" I call out as our resident town gossip and fellow witch shows up for her usual 6:30 AM breakfast burrito and coffee.

"Hello to you dear," Gladys responds, pausing only to remove her gloves and adjust her matching hat. Today's ensemble is a baby blue pillbox hat with a tiny faux bird perched on top. Gladys Miller, a tall thin witch, with a shock of unruly gray hair, always dresses to impress.

"All ready for spring today, I see."

"You noticed!" she responds, proudly snapping her gloves shut in her purse. "I'll have the usual."

I'm not sure why she bothers to request this. Damien prepares her daily vegan breakfast burrito at precisely 6:27. And it's always ready when she enters the café at 6:30. If she ever failed to show up, we'd go looking for her.

I inherited my grandmother's vegetarian breakfast café after she passed away last year. I never planned to return to Crested Peaks, but the thought of letting my grandmother's dream go was unbearable, so here I am.

I also inherited her demanding and feisty, helicopter-eared, ginger and white rabbit familiars: Marshall and Marcus. The café is actually named after them: Marcall's Breakfast Café.

"What's fresh on the news front?" I ask. And by news, I mean gossip. Laugh if you must, but Gladys' ear for gossip helped solve a murder last year and kept me out of jail.

"Rumor has it that two reality tv stars are hiding out in Old Man Finley's place. They've been there for several weeks."

"Get outta here! Which show?"

"That one where the young fella dates a whole bunch of women at once and then picks one to marry at the end."

"Wait, I watch that one. So, hang on a second, who exactly is staying in Old Man Finley's place?"

"I didn't catch the specific names, but they told me it was the young fella, and then the contestant who came in 4th place." Then Gladys shrugs like she could care less about the specifics.

She delivered the gossip and that's as far as she goes. Her job is done. "Does that mean anything to you?" she asks when she notices my shocked face.

"Gladys are you sure? They didn't say the winner?"

"Oh, they definitely didn't say that. It wasn't the winner, I'm positive they said 4th place. From your expression, that's clearly a surprise."

"Because he's supposed to be engaged to the winner!" I exclaim after I remove my hand from my mouth. I'm trying so hard not to shriek out loud and startle the other customers. It's a bit early for that. "If he's hiding out in the mountains with the 4th place girl something went seriously wrong."

Gladys shrugs again. "I don't make the news; I just report it."

"If the fans knew that the two of them are hiding in Crested Peaks, they'd go nuts."

"Who's hiding in Crested Peaks?" Damien asks as he appears from the kitchen with Gladys' burrito.

"Your second favorite reality tv star might be hiding at Old Man Finley's place with the Final 4 girl."

Damien nearly drops the burrito. "You're kidding me."

"That's what Gladys heard."

"That's huge!"

"I know!" I nearly shriek again. This is a lot of excitement to endure at 6:30 in the morning.

"Wow Gladys," Damien says, beaming at her in disbelief and admiration. "You always bring the goods."

"So do you!" she replies, snatching the burrito from him and hurrying to her favorite spot next to the window so she can watch everything happening outside. Did I mention Gladys takes her role as town gossip seriously?

I look up when the bell for the front door chimes again and it's my boyfriend, Detective Andrew Bailey who doesn't have supernatural abilities like me. He's just a top-notch detective. We were almost high school sweethearts, but his family disapproved of mine.

Which I actually didn't know until I returned to Crested Peaks last year. I spent ten years convinced that he thought I was an awful kisser. Turns out I just had horrible parents. My parents were Supernaturals, but they were also con artists who were killed by another crook when I was very young. Yeah, it's complicated.

"Detective Bailey," Gladys beams. "What a pleasant surprise. What brings you here on this bright spring morning?"

"I just happened to be passing by and thought I'd stop in for a Damien Special."

Damien flushes with pride. He's made no secret of the fact he thinks Drew is H.O.T. as he likes to say. Despite being married to his husband Tom for ten years. Who also agrees my boyfriend is oh so dreamy.

Yeah, I know, it's kind of annoying, really. They all think he's hot.

"Good morning, Gladys," he flashes her his patented megawatt grin.

"Catch any bad guys yet today?"

"Nobody yet, but the day is still young."

"You're doing a fine job, young man. Although I do wish you'd wear your uniform more often. I appreciate a man in uniform."

Drew chuckles good naturedly. "I'm a detective now Gladys. I'm no longer a beat cop in uniform."

"I suppose," Gladys sighs while I roll my eyes in the background. All this adoration just makes him cockier and bossier than he needs to be. He hated that I insisted on investigating the crime that threatened to put me in jail for a murder I didn't commit.

"Leave this to the professionals, Char" he kept telling me. The body was discovered right behind my café. And all because there were secret tunnels underneath here that no one (well almost no one) knew about.

I refused to just leave it to the professionals whose focus was on me nearly the entire time.

"Here you go Drew, your Damien Special."

"Aw, thanks Damien, you're the best."

Damien puffs his chest out at the compliment but as he turns to leave, he catches the noticeable eye roll I've aimed in his direction and sticks out his tongue before heading back to the kitchen.

"What are you 12?" I taunt.

"Maybe!" he yells back.

The Damien Special is a black bean breakfast burrito that my Cuban-born chef created and is famous throughout the ski area. It's a special recipe and even I don't know exactly what's in it. I do know it's a mixture of eggs, beans, cheese, potatoes, grilled jalapenos, and caramelized onions, all layered with a secret sauce. It's so amazing that people are convinced I conjured up some kind of magic to make them, but I swear it's all Damien.

Drew digs into his burrito while Damien happily returns to the kitchen to make another delicious creation. Marshall and Marcus hop out of the kitchen with their feline friend Stumpy close on their heels. "Hey lady."

"Yes?" I respond, looking down at the trio in wonder. I don't know why they still insist on calling me lady, but now I'm used to it. Along with my grandmother's café and house, I somehow inherited her ability to communicate with them.

I'm the only one who can hear them, so I have to relay their messages to everyone else. And yes, that was an awkward conversation to have with the new boyfriend.

I refused to tell Drew for the longest time, but I finally fessed up after way too many close calls. And even though their ability to talk makes Damien nervous, Drew is convinced that eventually, he'll be able to hear them as well.

Before you get too excited, though, I'm not Dr. Doolittle or anything, and I don't talk to all the animals. I can't communicate with their cat friend, but they can, pass on his messages to me.

He lives in the restaurant next door, which used to be an Italian restaurant until the owner was also murdered last year. Rita, the landlord of our building, is still looking for a new tenant the last time I checked. But I'm not sure where Stumpy will go if they kick him out.

They look up at me while waggling their crooked ears. "Stumpy says he found a dead body under some bushes in Snowball Park."

They tell me this so casually like these things happen all the time in Crested Peaks. "Really, and what was Stumpy doing in the park?" I ask, somewhat dubious of their claim.

"Looking for mice."

"Okay, and what did this dead body look like?"

Drew glances up from his breakfast with a raised eyebrow at the word body. I shrug at him, still somewhat doubtful about all of this.

"He says it's a man whose face is covered in blood. He smelled him and he's certain he's dead."

Er, now I'm a little concerned and I look over at Drew. "What is it?" he asks.

"Stumpy claims there's a body in Snowball Park, under the bushes, with blood on his face."

Chapter 2

"Are you sure?" Drew asks, his face registering a mixture of hopeful disbelief and concern. If there is a body in the park, and he brushes this off, his captain will have his hide.

"They don't normally kid about these things," I start. "I know it's hard to imagine there's an actual body in there." My shoulders slump in resignation. "I certainly hope there's no body, but I don't think Stumpy is making this up. Perhaps he's just mistaken about what he saw."

Drew sighs and puts his hands on his hips while staring at the three of them, no doubt thinking he can intimidate them into telling the truth. When they continue to stare back, he shakes his head, sighing again. "I'll check it out just in case," he responds, yanking his radio off his hip. "This is 20 Victor. I've got a possible body in Snowball Park. Requesting a patrol car for assistance."

"Copy that 20 Victor, 20 Adam responding, we're about three minutes out."

"Roger that," Drew says, shoving his radio back in its holster.

I catch Gladys ogling him while he's acting all official. I can certainly understand why. Even I think he's extra handsome when he acts all policey in front of me. I mean, when he's not lecturing me about interfering in an investigation, that is. But I know firsthand how hard it is to tear myself away from those intense green eyes. They get me every time.

"Let's go check out a dead body," I insist as I take off my apron.

He holds up his hand, blocking my path to the front door. "Whoa. Let's nothing. This is official police business. We don't know what's really out there. You stay put."

"Oh c'mon." I pout. "I promise I'll stay in the background, and you won't even know I'm there. It's my rabbits who provided the information after all."

"Technically, it was the cat," he points to Stumpy who responds with a swish of his extra-long tail. "And I can't believe I just said that," he adds with a grimace.

I understand, the whole talking animals, witchcraft thing is hard to get used to. He knew I was a witch, considering my grandmother and my parents were. But the talking animal thing really threw him for a loop.

For many years, I felt like if I refused to use witchcraft, I wouldn't turn into criminals like my parents. What I didn't realize at the time was that they weren't con artists because they were Supernatural. They were just con artists, period.

It wasn't until I returned to Crested Peaks that I chose to embrace my abilities, albeit reluctantly at first. My best friend Miranda, who owns the Bean Around A Bit Coffee Shop across the street, is helping me hone my talents.

And I have to admit, if it weren't for my being a witch, I probably would have been killed by the murderer I apprehended last year. Ever since then, I've been discovering just how fun and useful witchcraft is.

But back to the alleged body in the park. I push Drew's hand away and move toward the door again. "Yes, but if it weren't for my rabbits' ability to communicate with me, you wouldn't know about this at all."

He sighs a third time, and I know I've got him. "You're just going to follow me as soon as I leave anyway, aren't you?"

I nod my head.

"Fine. But stay out of the way. I'm not sure what's actually out there until I see it. I don't want you taking any chances."

"Yes sir, I promise you won't even notice I'm there. Hey Damien!" I shout back to the kitchen. "Keep an eye on the place, would you? I'm going to check on a possible body!"

"Sure thing!" he shouts back.

He clearly doesn't believe me, or he'd be worried and tell me I should let Drew investigate alone. Then when he realized, like Drew, that he couldn't stop me, he'd beg me to be careful. To be certain I don't really think there's a dead body. I think maybe Stumpy is confused. But I'm still curious enough to check it out.

I follow Drew out the door, but as promised, I keep my distance. Snowball Park is a short walk from the café, and the patrol car pulls up just as we arrive.

"I'm told there may be a body under the bushes on the west side," Drew says as he points toward the area. We all walk that direction, but it's obvious even from way back here, that there's something big lying on the ground. Drew motions for me to drop back. Could Stumpy be right?

He and the patrolmen move in closer to check it out up close. I notice how they follow his lead quickly and without question. At over six feet tall, sporting his usual short, no-nonsense haircut, he cuts an imposing figure.

My pulse races when he scowls and plucks his radio from his belt again. "Dispatch, this is 20 Victor; we have a body with what appears to be a gunshot wound to the head. I need someone from homicide and the ME's office on the northwest corner of Snowball Park."

Holy crap. Stumpy was right. And maybe even murder? Drew marches over to me. "This place is about to be swarming with cops. You go back to work."

Ugh. He can be so bossy at times. Like he forgets, not everybody works for him. But another body? This is unbelievable. "Was he murdered?"

"I won't know more until we investigate the scene, so please, do me a favor and go back to Marcall's."

"Okay, call me if you need anything," I tell him reluctantly. I know when I've pushed it as far as I can, and anything more will just make him grumpier than ever.

"Will do." His face is grim as he returns to his duties.

A body with a gunshot wound. And when I came back to Crested Peaks, I thought this place would be boring.

I trudge back to the café, the rabbits and Stumpy trailing behind. I repeatedly turn back to watch the patrolmen wind bright yellow crime scene tape around the area and shoo away the growing crowd of gawkers.

Why can't I be a gawker and just watch from the sidelines? Why do I have to be the one to leave the crime scene? Probably because if the last murder was any indication, I'll somehow find myself accidentally involved anyway.

Damien barely looks up when I walk through the front door. "Hey, how was the dead body?"

"They're putting up crime scene tape now. They're thinking gun shot."

Then his eyes practically bug out of his head. "What? You were serious? I thought you were just sneaking off to make out with Detective McHotty."

"No!" I fire back. "Stumpy told the rabbits he saw a dead body in the park, so we went to verify it. McHotty—I mean Drew - said it looks like a gunshot wound."

"That's horrible! Is it someone we know?"

"He didn't say, but I have to think if it was, he would have reacted a little differently."

"I can't believe that. And if it's murder, that's the third one we've had since you came back. What's up with that?"

"Very funny." I glare at him, although I'm secretly wondering the same thing.

When I was in grade school, I had this friend whose grandpa hated Angela Lansbury because of the show Murder She Wrote. For sure, Grandpa wasn't all there and couldn't always separate fact from fiction.Still, he liked to point out that wherever Jessica Fletcher went, people died. He wasn't wrong ,and it always made me giggle. But now I'm feeling a bit like Jessica Fletcher myself.

I'm still barely in the cafe when Miranda bursts through the door like she often does when she has news to share or at least thinks we do. "Have you heard? There's --"

"--a dead body in the park!" Damien and I respond in unison.

"Dang, I guess you have," she laughs. "You two are downright scary, I hope you know. So, what happened exactly? One of my customers just said it's a guy with an ax buried in his head."

"What?" I laugh. "There's no ax. He was shot."

"How do you know that? Oh. Never mind. Detective McHotty is on the case, and you have the inside scoop, don't you?"

"I walked to the park with him after Stumpy told us he saw a body in the bushes. But that's all I know."

Miranda glares at me while tapping her foot in annoyance. She's shorter than I am. Although at five feet 10 inches, almost everyone is shorter than I am, except Drew. She likes to wear her hair short and spikey, and today it's colored a playful springtime yellow. "So, you knew firsthand there was a body in Snowball Park, and you didn't come and get me?"

"There wasn't time Drew called it in and then went to check it out. I was ordered to stay out of the way and keep quiet. I really don't know anything more, except that it's a body with a gunshot wound."

"Is it somebody we know?"

"I don't think so."

"This is crazy. Another dead body in Crested Peaks."

I'm beginning to take this personally.

Before we can discuss the latest mystery any further, an unexpected rush of spring skiers flows into the shop, and they're extra hungry. We've done a brisk business this week with the unseasonably warm weather.

Spring skiing doesn't always feature the best snow, but the tourists are eager to bask in our famous Colorado sunshine. You can even spot the occasional skier wearing shorts this time of year. I'm never convinced it's warm enough for that, but to each his own. As long as they keep coming in here to eat, I don't care what they wear on the slopes.

There's also a sharp increase in hungry tourists and townsfolk alike today with the police activity in the park. The best part is the stories get more outrageous as the morning wears on. People are convinced they alone have the inside track. They lean in and whisper to me that they have it on very good authority that it's a famous football player/rockstar/actor, who was killed.

They go on to tell me that the famous person died from a variety of causes: strangulation, beating, stabbing. There are some very active imaginations in our little mountain town. At this rate, they may even solve the Kennedy assassination mystery.

I keep hoping I'll hear from Drew about the case, but by late afternoon, as we get ready to close, I give up and have to assume that he's busy and he'll call me when he gets the chance. If it really is a murder, he'll have his hands full. "Way to go boss." Damien pats me on the back as I magically change the Open sign to Closed. "Business was great today!"

"I feel kind of bad though that a sizeable piece of that business came from a body in the park."

"Have you heard anything new from Drew?"

"Nope. Not a peep. But I'm sure he's already working overtime, solving the case."

"If you don't need anything else, I'll go home now. Bubbles will undoubtedly be looking for a walk. But let me know if you hear anything, okay?"

Bubbles is Damien and Tom's rescued pibble. The best part is, she acts like a dog named Bubbles should act. She's hilarious. Damien's mother-in-law keeps hinting she'd like a human grandchild as well, but so far, he and Tom have been tight lipped about any children.

Just as I'm about to tell him to have a good evening, he pauses with his hand on the door. "I can trust you right?"

"Of course, you can! But with what?" I ask.

"I can trust that as soon as I walk out of here, you won't run over to the park and snoop around?"

Now I'm annoyed. "Did Drew tell you to say that?"

"No, Drew didn't say a word to me, but I know how you get, and now I'm worried that you're going to put yourself right in the middle of this whole thing. You could have been killed last time boss, and I don't want anything to happen to you." Damien's eyes are pleading.

"If it makes you feel any better, I have paperwork that, as much as I'd like it to just finish itself, I haven't been able to come up with a spell that does that. So yes, you can trust that I won't sprint to the park the minute you're gone, just to see what I can dig up. Okay?"

"Well, okay," Damien concedes reluctantly.

Besides, what he doesn't know is I've been sneaking peeks in that direction all day and the police are gone, along with what I assume is any evidence that might be worth finding. At this point I'll just have to wait until I hear something new from Drew.

"You go home and take Bubbles for an extra-long walk, and I'll see you tomorrow morning."

"Okay," he grumbles as he slowly leaves the café, repeatedly turning back to make sure I'm staying put like I said I would. I finally click the door shut and lock it. He worries too much.

When I see him try to peek back around the corner through the window at me, I put my hands around my mouth and call out, "Go home Damien!" I laugh and shake my head at him when he scampers away.

Chapter 3

After finishing some of the dreaded office paperwork, I call out to the rabbits hoping they're here, and not out begging for treats from someone. Otherwise, I'll have to walk up and down Main Street to track them down. I told them not to interfere in the police investigation in the park, but if they happened to overhear anything important, they should feel free to let me know.

"Marshall, Marcus, it's time to go home!"

The two of them scamper out of the supply closet, where they probably spent most of the day napping. But as we stroll through the parking lot to my ancient Prius, I notice that Stumpy the cat from next door, is following us.

I assume when he realizes we're going home, he'll turn back, but he doesn't. He blinks up at me, patiently waiting for me to open the car door. When I do, the rabbits hop in, and I bend down to get on his level. "Honey, don't you think you should go back home?"

I don't really expect a response since so far, I can only converse with my rabbit familiars, but there's no reason to be a jerk and just say, "Shoo!"

"We told him he could come home with us," Marcus explains.

"But he already has a home," I remind him.

"Not anymore. The new renter for Tony's old restaurant said if he didn't leave, he'd have to go to the shelter. Whatever that is. She told him she didn't want some mangy old 2-footed cat hanging around all the time. It didn't sound like a place Stumpy would like, so I told him he could live with us."

These rabbits can be exasperating. "Do you think you should have asked me first?"

"Nah."

"Hang on a second. Did you say there's a new renter for Tony's place?"

"We did," they respond in unison.

"Why didn't you tell me this earlier? When did you find out?"

"You didn't ask," Marshall tells me in response to the first question.

"Today," Marcus answers the second.

They're so literal. Sometimes I wonder why I even bother. But while both rabbits have jumped into the passenger seat, Stumpy remains on the ground looking up at me expectantly.

"What's he doing?" I ask the rabbits.

"He needs you to pick him up because he can't jump very high on account of his stumps. Also, we'll need to get some step stools for him so he can get up on the couch and the bed."

"Well of course we will." I stand there, hands on my hips, looking down at this ridiculous cat while I ponder my options. He looks at me in such a pathetic way I'm convinced he practiced it just for the occasion. When he tilts his head at me, I know they've won, but I refuse to admit it.

I turn to the rabbits. "You guys, we don't really need another mou-" I stop when they give me the exact same pathetic look. Now I know they all practiced it. I throw my hands up in defeat. "Fine!"

I pick up the cat and put him in the passenger seat with them. They're obviously used to getting their way, and they're the only living reminder I have left of my Gran. But do they have to be such pushy little old men?

"What do cats even eat," I wonder out loud as I make my way to the unexpected pit stop at the store.

"I think mice," Marshall informs me.

"I'm not getting mice for him to eat. He can eat cat food like every other feline out there."

After I pull into the parking spot and open the door to get out, all three of them leap into my lap, then scramble to the pavement below. "Oh no, that's where I draw the line. You three aren't allowed in the grocery store."

As usual, they ignore me and continue their steady jog toward the front door. "Don't blame me if they kick you out!" I call after them. It's crazy enough that I inherited the two rabbits, but now I'll have a cat?

He was instrumental in helping me catch both killers last year, though. And I hate the thought of him sitting in the shelter all by himself. Ugh. I can't believe I have a cat now.

When I reach the front door, I find the three of them waiting for me. "Hurry up you slow poke!" Marcus insists.

I shake my head in disbelief that this is my life and grab the nearest shopping cart while they continue to watch me expectantly. "What is it now?"

"Stumpy wants to ride in the shopping cart," Marshall informs me.

"Are you kidding me?" Once again, the three of them stare up at me pleadingly. This is getting to be a problem. I sigh loudly and bend down to scoop them up, one by one, and place them in the shopping cart. I swear if we don't get thrown out for this, it will be a miracle. In fact, it would serve them right.

Instead, the grocery store employees don't even notice, while all the shoppers stop to ooh and ah, and these three characters play right along. If only these people knew what they were really like.

As I trudge through the produce section, Marshall and Marcus call out requests. "Get some parsley! We can never have enough parsley!"

"What about cilantro?" I respond.

"Bleah!" Marshall says as he shudders and sticks out his tongue.

"You're a rabbit. How can you not like cilantro?"

"It's genetic," Marcus explains.

When Marshall scowls at Stumpy and asks him, "How can you not know what a blueberry tastes like?" I decide I'm never going shopping with these three again. This is just too weird.

When a familiar man walks past us, glances in the cart, smiles, and chuckles softly, I'm desperate to remember how I know him. Is he a regular at Marcalls? Does he work at the bank? Argh! How do I know this guy? Think brain, think!

It takes me all the way to the pet food section when I get the answer. It's the bachelor! From tv! How did I not know that? Damien will be furious I didn't get a picture for him. What doesn't Glady's know?

***

Later that night, while watching tv with Stumpy, who's curled up next to me on the couch snoring softly, I finally get a text from Drew.

Drew: Sorry for the late text. I've been working non-stop today, but I promise I'll make it up to you tomorrow. You won't believe how this case is shaping up.

Rats. I'm disappointed, but I'm getting used to life as a cop's girl-friend. Drew works a lot. And often weird hours. He doesn't always get nights and weekends off.

But now I'm really curious about what's going on with the case. I don't think it's anyone we know because I'm sure he would have already told me that. But what exactly could have him this busy and secretive?

Chapter 4

The next morning, just as a teeny tiny sliver of sun cracks on the horizon, the four of us get into my car and head to the cafe. It wasn't until I ran a breakfast café that I realized what the phrase "crack of dawn" meant.

Really what it means is that it's all I can do to stumble to my car and drive to the café in the dark, and hope Damien gets the coffee going quickly so I can wake up. This morning though, I notice how the slightly warmer spring air feels on my face. I detect the ever so faint scent of spring blossoms and hear the birds who are also waking up while warming up their vocal cords. The crack of dawn in spring is a lot easier to tolerate than the crack of dawn in a snowstorm.

And yet, the burden of another body in Crested Peaks weighs on me. I still haven't heard anything new from Drew, and there was only a tiny blurb on the internet this morning about a body in the park. It said they're withholding names until relatives can be notified.

Nothing about a murder and nothing about a gunshot wound. I assume the police are being tight-lipped for a reason.

As soon as I pull up to Marcall's, and open the car door for them, the three boys jostle over who gets out first to start their search for today's adventure.

"I'm going to find a body today!" Marshall insists, elbowing his brother right between the eyes.

"Oof." Marcus grunts shoving him back so hard he tumbles from the passenger seat onto the parking lot.

"Jerk!" He mutters under his breath as he stomps his foot and then works furiously to clean his ears of imaginary dust, he's convinced he received in the tumble. "Well, I'm going to find my own body!" He declares as they both head for the park.

"C'mon Stumpy! Let's see what's out there!" They both eagerly beckon to their friend.

"How about no one finds any bodies anywhere, okay?" I call out after their retreating backs. I put my hands on my face and sigh. What a weird life I have now.

While I don't know exactly how old the rabbits are, they must be ancient. My grandmother always insisted that she won them in a poker game many decades ago, and they've been in the family ever since.

So far, Gran and I are the only ones they've communicated with. Considering your basic pet rabbit, as adorable as they are, only lives around ten years. And they definitely don't talk. So I have always lived under the assumption these two are magical in more ways than one.

As for Stumpy, he claims he's a war veteran who lost most of his back legs in an unfortunate enemy ambush. I'm not sure how true that is. He actually gets around remarkably well for a two-legged cat. And now I guess he's part of the family too. He's certainly not as cantankerous as the rabbits, so he has that going for him.

Damien pulls up right after we do. "Girl!" he shouts out his car window. "I can't believe you didn't call me last night! What's going on with the dead guy?"

I throw my hands in the air. "I know about as much as you do. I only got a text from Drew saying I'd never believe what's going on."

"That sounds bad."

"My thoughts exactly. He said he'd make it up to me today, which better include filling me in on everything."

While Damien busies himself with the day's menu items, and I wrap the silverware in colorful napkins, I suddenly remember I never told him about the trip to the grocery store. He's going to kill me.

"Sooooo, you'll never guess who I saw at the grocery store last night."

"The bachelor."

I gasp. "How did you know?"

His hands stop his food prep midair. He looks up at me slowly. Uh oh. "I was joking."

"Oh." I smile my most placating smile. "Uhhh I wasn't."

"You saw a reality tv star, here in Crested Peaks, in the grocery store last night, and you're just now telling me?" Every word is emphasized in a measured tone. "Since you didn't bother to call me, while in the store, I assume you at least got me a picture."

After seeing the guilty look on my face, he continues. "Tell me you got a picture, so I don't have to quit right here and now."

"I'm so sorry Damien! To be fair, it took me several minutes to realize who he was! He walked by me in the produce section and laughed when he saw Marshall, Marcus, and Stumpy in the cart! For a second, I thought maybe he was a regular here or something. I'm so sorry!"

Fortunately, for a moment, he just looks confused, hopefully forgetting my transgression. "Why were you in the grocery store with those three in a grocery cart? Are you sure you didn't just dream this?"

"It's a long story, but Stumpy lives with us now thanks to the rabbits, and we were in the grocery store getting food for all three of them."

Damien shakes his head in disbelief. "That is such a weird story that I'm not sure what to say for now. But you owe me," he insists as he points a wooden spoon at me.

Never mess with a chef wielding a wooden spoon. "I agree." I raise my hands in surrender. "And I swear it will never happen again." Except when I remember the other thing. "Wait! One more thing I forgot."

"Are you kidding me?"

"The rabbits said there's a new tenant for Tony's old place. That's kind of why Stumpy is living with us now. And before you ask," I add because that's obviously what's coming next, "I don't know who they are or what they'll be doing." Okay, there. I've told him everything I can remember. I just need to keep him from quitting on me.

Damien returns to his morning prep muttering in Spanish. I'm pretty sure I don't want to know what he's saying. By the time we open, there's a line of hungry people waiting for their breakfast burritos.

Several of them are clutching coffee cups they got at Miranda's shop across the street. Business is brisk the first hour ,and the customers are still talking about the body from the park.

Finally, after what seems like forever, but is really only about an hour and a half, Drew walks in the café, and he's obviously been up all night.

"You look like you need a bucket of coffee."

"That bad huh?" he grimaces, rubbing his hand across an unshaven chin.

"Nah, I hear the sexy, devil-may-care look is in these days."

He crooks one eyebrow. "Sexy? Maybe I should work all night more often."

"Do you want me to ask Damien to make a pot of coffee for you? Or I could run across the street to Miranda's and get some."

"What I could really use is some breakfast and a big glass of oj. And then a shower."

"I can definitely get you breakfast and juice, but as for showers, we took those out just last week. People kept leaving their towels on the floor, and it was a nuisance."

"Ah, just my luck. What's the special of the day?"

I rub my hands together and grin. "Damien has prepared a sweet potato, black bean, egg, and avocado burrito. How does that sound?"

"That sounds amazing!" he moans. "Throw in some hash browns, too, would you?"

"Hey Damien!" I shout back to the kitchen. "Drew wants the day's special with hash browns!"

"Coming right up!"

I know Damien will insist on hearing what Drew says anyway, so I fill him in on the latest news about how Stumpy now lives with me, courtesy of the rabbits.

Drew watches me pour him a large glass of orange juice. "Don't tell me the cat talks to you now too."

"No, he's still only talking to the rabbits."

"And he told them about the body, so they told you."

I respond with a smile. I realize how absurd this all sounds, and I was raised with it.

"Do you know how hard it is to come up with stories to tell my boss about how you learned of certain things?"

I pat him on the shoulder. "Welcome to my world."

Damien whips the burrito and hashbrowns together in record time and plops the platter down in front of Drew. "Did I miss anything?"

"Nope. I was just telling him about Stumpy."

"Oh good," he says as the two of us turn to Drew, eager for him to spill. He narrows his eyes as he regards the two of us crowding the counter staring at him.

"Is it all right if I eat a few bites first? Or do I have to starve just to satisfy your curiosity?"

"Eat!" Damien urges.

"Starve!" I insist.

"Seriously?" Damien throws back at me as I stand up to tall, hoping to intimidate him. My height beats his shortness every time. He plants his hands on his hips and glares up at me. I may have a good five inches on him, but the customers don't eat without him, so I back down like I always do where he's concerned.

"Fine. Eat." I grumble.

My stocky and brilliant chef slowly shakes his head.

"What?" I put my hands up. "I need to know!"

"You know I don't have to tell you anything. I probably shouldn't tell you half of what I do," Drew reminds me with a mouth half stuffed with burrito.

"Go on, eat. I don't want you to have to talk with a mouth full of food or anything."

Drew continues to shovel burrito and hashbrowns into his mouth like he hasn't eaten since yesterday. Which, come to think of it, maybe he hasn't. He gets so busy he forgets to eat. Me. I live to eat. I guess it's a good thing I own a breakfast café.

After several more bites Drew finally tires of watching the two of us hang over him like vultures counting every bite. He finally puts his half-eaten burrito down on the plate. "Okay, here's the deal. You can't tell anyone else what I'm about to tell you. I'm serious, okay? There's a reason we haven't made any of this public. The body we found in the park yesterday belongs to Vinny 'Bubblegum' Rossini."

Drew pauses for dramatic effect. He expects us to be shocked. Maybe even horrified.

Instead, we meet his revelation with peals of laughter.

"What's so funny?" Drew looks aghast.

"Bubblegum!" I squeal as we break into laughter again.

"You make it sound like he's some kind of mobster," Damien titters. "Ohhhh Vinny 'Bubblegum' Rossini is in town. Look out everybody."

Drew glares at us like we're children he caught whispering in class. Then he calmly takes another bite of his burrito. "That's because he is."

"Is what?" I ask. I still don't get this.

"A mobster," Drew replies, swigging his orange juice.

"You're serious?" Damien asks.

"He got the nickname 'Bubblegum' from the fact he's never without gum. And he's a high-level operative in the Calazzo crime family syndicate. One of the FBI's most wanted for over a decade."

Damien blanches at the news. "What is the mafia doing in Crested Peaks?"

"That's exactly what we're trying to figure out. And why order a hit on him? Was it a rival crime family? An internal hit? We don't know."

"No wonder you were so busy last night!"

"And the FBI is breathing down our necks on top of everything else."

I gulp. "Now you're scaring me. What is the mafia doing in Crested Peaks?" I reach for Drew's orange juice; my mouth has suddenly gone dry.

Damien looks confused. "Did anyone report any gunshots the night it happened? Because that's one story I haven't heard yet."

I nod my head in agreement. Out of all the wild and crazy theories we've heard the last couple of days, none of them have included hearing gunfire.

"It appears they used a silencer. And no," Drew continues giving me that steely eyed glare I'm all too familiar with, "I can already see the wheels turning." Then he actually waggles his finger at me for emphasis.

"Stay out of this Char. This is very dangerous. Vinny is wanted for killing dozens of men and women who appeared to betray the Calazzos. Whoever got to him is probably worse. Do not stick your nose into this."

I can't believe he's shaking his finger at me like I'm a child. "I was only wondering, that's all."

"Make sure that's all it is. I mean it."

After Drew finishes his breakfast, he thanks Damien for the delicious and much needed meal. Then he warns me one more time to stay out of the investigation before heading home to shower.

Chapter 5

Right on cue, Miranda rushes into Marcall's after Drew leaves. It's basically her signature move. Interesting how she usually avoids getting in trouble with Drew that way. She's out of breath from sprinting across the street. I can even picture her dodging cars on Main Street in her haste. "What did he say?"

I glance over at Damien. In all the excitement, we kind of forgot Miranda would want to know.

"Oh, c'mon you guys! You know you can tell me. We're a team."

"Drew has to know we'd tell Miranda," Damien points out.

"True," I admit reluctantly. "The body they found belonged to some high-level mobster. Like a big deal kind of FBI most wanted type. And now the CPPD and the FBI need to figure out why he was in Crested Peaks. And they also need to know why someone else would want to kill him."

"A wise guy. In Crested Peaks? That's just bizarre." Miranda looks like she almost doesn't believe us, and I don't blame her.

"Wise guy?" I ask. "You've been binge watching cops shows again, haven't you?"

"Maybe," she says as she stubbornly crosses her arms over her chest in defiance. Busted! If Netflix charged by the episode, she'd be broke.

"But yes, that was my thought too," I respond, nodding my head vigorously. "What could the mafia want with this town?"

"You mean aside from the year-round breathtaking scenery and epic skiing through fresh powder on a crystal-clear winter morning?" Damien butts in.

We both turn to him with quizzical looks. Miranda finally answers, "I'm guessing that isn't a big draw for organized crime Mr. Travel Brochure."

I throw up my hands. "I have no idea."

"Maybe diamonds!" Miranda exclaims.

I laugh at first but pause when I see she's serious. "Diamonds? In Colorado? A state that was pretty much founded on the Gold Rush? We don't have diamonds here." I'm convinced Miranda has us mixed up with some other place. Like an entirely different country. "Do we?"

"The Colorado mountains are actually full of gems, according to Miles. Diamonds, sapphires, opals, peridot, lots of good stuff."

Miles is the town librarian and a Colorado history buff. Plus he's Miranda's boyfriend, so if she got her background from him maybe she doesn't have it mixed up after all.

"How come I've never heard about any of this?"

"You'd have to ask Miles for more details, but when he was explaining it to me once, he said part of the reason no one knows about the gemstones is that you can't just walk up a mountain peak and then dig for diamonds. They're well protected by nature."

Damien tosses me a sponge to wipe down some of the dirty tables in the dining room. "She has a point."

"Why don't you just magic them clean?" Miranda asks as I scrub at a particularly stubborn spot of ketchup.

"It helps me think," I explain while I move on to a puddle of spilled orange juice. "I toured the train museum last month, and they said hundreds, if not thousands, of people died in the quest for gold, and many more just gave up and turned back because the untamed mountains were too harsh."

"Plus, as Miles tells me, most of the mountains are federally protected. Even if you had easy access, the gems aren't just there for the taking." Miranda adds.

Damien scrunches up his face. "I don't know, it still seems so unlikely that the mob would come to Colorado for diamonds. That's more like a plot line from a movie."

"Hey, don't look at me, I just work here!" Miranda responds. "And speaking of working, I should get back to the shop. We've been swamped lately, but I wanted to buzz over here and see if you had any news."

I waggle the sponge at her. "Promise you won't discuss this with anyone else. Damian and I are already under strict orders not to share what we know."

"My lips are sealed!" Miranda sings as she sails out the door, making a zipper motion across her mouth.

Damien wanders back into the kitchen. "They say diamonds are a gay's best friend!"

"I'm pretty sure that's supposed to be girl's friend you derp," I call after him.

"Potato, puhtahto!" He sings.

"Now I think we should go sapphire hunting," I muse.

"Every once in a while, you still hear about someone accidentally coming across a gold nugget in one of the nearby rivers. This may sound weird, but you know what I think is kind of neat?" Damien pauses. "The idea that there is still some gold, or as Miranda said, even some diamonds or sapphires, buried deep within the Colorado mountains that no one can ever get to."

"You don't hope to dig them up yourself?" I ask.

"I really don't. It's like they're hidden in their own little mysterious place, and they'll just have to stay there. They don't have to be protected by the security guard at the museum like the ones they've already dug up. Or worn on some rich lady's ears. They're protected by mother nature and our majestic Rocky Mountains instead."

"I get that," I respond as I levitate a pile of dirty dishes back into the kitchen to be washed. Hey, I didn't say I never used magic to clean. Other people's dirty dishes are pretty much the worst after all.

"I still wouldn't mind finding a big ol' diamond that happened to float down a river and then sail down the gutter through town where I just happened to come across it one afternoon."

"Oh, you and me both, sister!" Damien laughs.

We're surprised when we hear shouting, mixed with drilling and hammering noises outside. We both scamper to the front window where we see a work truck bearing the sign "Signs R Us" on their door. The new tenants!

We rush outside to see what we can find out. Several workers are hoisting a sizeable wooden sign up to the front of the building: Alice's Tavern.

"Whoa," Damien gasps as we turn to each other excitedly. This looks promising! We're disappointed when the workmen shoo us away from the front of the building as we crane our necks and try to peer in the window and get a glimpse of the new owner.

"Outta dah way yuz two!" one of the workers shouts at us. "Are yuz blind? Dis sign is heavy! Could crush a person in dah blink of an eye if dey aint careful."

I try not to laugh as I recognize an accent I haven't heard since I left New York. Even though there was a time, shortly after inheriting my Gran's café, that I was convinced I wanted to move back there, that's long past. But the accent sure brings back memories.

Damien and I step back out of their way and continue to watch. The windows are still covered with butcher block paper inside, but it's been vacant for months, and we haven't seen even a hint of movement over here until now.

It's a bigger sign than most of the shops have along the street, and it takes two men to attach it to the front of the building while another stands below shouting orders.

But my head snaps upwards when I hear a loud creaking noise, and for a second, I feel powerless as I watch one of the pulleys break apart. The heavy sign gives way and rockets toward the man on the sidewalk.

I hear the men on the ladder shout to the one on the ground. He stares up at the massive block of wood that's bearing down on him, but he's cemented to the spot.

I concentrate hard and manage to throw him a few feet to his left. It isn't pretty, but when the sign crashes to the ground, instead of on him I let out of whoosh of air I didn't realize I'd been holding in. The man on the ground lumbers to his feet while the other two scramble down the ladders to reach him.

"Duke! Are you okay?"

"Uhhh yeah, I think so. I skinned up my elbow, but it's better than getting hit by that sign."

"I had no idea you could move so fast!" the second man exclaims.

The man on the ground laughs nervously, "Yeah, neither did I."

"C'mon you guys we better get the sign up before Alice gets here."

"You sure you're okay dude? That was a close call."

"Yeah, yeah, I'm good. Let's get back to work." All three of them are visibly shaken, and the man I threw aside is pale, but at least they look like they're okay. Onlookers gather, trying to figure out what all the commotion was.

Damien turns to me, "I take it you're not going to tell them?"

I brush it off, "Nope."

"That guy could have been injured really bad. Or even killed! You saved him Charlotte."

"That's okay. I don't need credit. Especially since I pretty much threw him into the ground. It would have been more impressive if I'd been able to stop the sign in the first place."

"Whatever you say boss. I still think you did an amazing thing."

"I'm dying to meet the new tenant!" I change the subject as Damien and I slowly return to Marcall's.

"At least we know what kind of place it will be now. I bet they'll have beer and burgers."

"And french fries!" I add.

Chapter 6

Shortly before closing, I'm on my hands and knees rearranging one of the lower shelves under the cash register when I hear the door chime, so I peer over the top of the counter. "Good afternoon!" I greet our newest customer. "Welcome to Marcall's."

She's an older woman whose long silver hair perches atop her head in a messy bun. The numerous bracelets she wears on each wrist jangle merrily. Her tie-dyed t-shirt and long swirling purple skirt complete the look perfectly. "Hello there, new neighbor!"

I smile. "Are you Alice by any chance?"

"In the flesh!" She greets me with a half curtsy and her bracelets jangle some more. "Are you Charlotte?"

"I am!"

"I've been eager to meet you! Rita told me you have a vegetarian breakfast cafe."

"I sure do, it was my grandmother's, but she passed away last year, and I inherited it."

"I'm from Chicago where I also run the original Alice's Tavern, but I decided it was time to get out of the city and live in a place where I could actually relax once in a while. Take up hiking or fishing or whatever seems appropriate. Maybe I'll even learn to snowboard."

I like this Alice person. "And I notice you've already adopted the appropriate lingo."

"Oh yes, my grandson told me about that. The crucial difference between skiing and snowboarding. He said one should not mix up the two for fear of some kind of nameless, but harsh penalty."

Sadly, she's right. "And I don't ski or snowboard, so I can't really help you there, but we often have instructors who come in here to eat, so if you're looking for one next winter, they'll be easy to find."

She claps her hands together excitedly. "Delightful! I know I'll love it here."

"When do you hope to open?"

"Tomorrow!"

"Tomorrow?" I'm completely confused. How is that possible? They haven't even moved in yet. The only thing they've done is install the sign.

"I bet you're wondering how that's possible, aren't you?" She asks, a mischievous glint in her eye.

"I am. You haven't moved anything in yet."

"But that's where you're wrong. Come take a look, dear."

I follow her out the door. This is puzzling news. The first activity we've seen at all over here, after they moved Tony's stuff out, was the new sign. How could they--

"Whoa!" I exclaim. "When did you move in?" The butcher block paper is torn down, and I can see the entire place has been redone in the style of a dark and rustic tavern. Gone are most of the Italian fine dining fixtures replaced with beer and liquor-themed signs, plus a bar in the center.

I don't think she's a Supernatural because I can usually tell. So how on earth could she have finished a complete remodel of Tony's old place without any of us knowing? And even if she was a witch, something of this magnitude would be incredibly difficult.

She sees the look of shock on my face and giggles, "My crew has been working at night all week, and they finished yesterday. We got lucky and secured all the permits in record time. We were just waiting for the transformation to be complete."

"That's great!" I tell her. "You must be very excited." Damien will never believe this. I still don't. He'll be mad he was at the supply store when she stopped by. She obviously has a heck of a crew to get something like this put together in a matter of days.

"Rita tells me you're a witch."

"I am!" I respond. It still feels a little strange to admit that so easily now. Not that I'm ashamed of being a witch. My Gran was a witch after all, but in my grandmother's day they kept it hidden for fear of reprisal.

But now, people find it rather interesting. And ever since I realized it was something to be proud of, I no longer hide it either. And yet I'm still a little surprised whenever it rolls of my tongue.

"Marvelous! I think we're going to have a lot of fun. Stop in soon and we'll have a beer together. I've recruited some of the very best Colorado breweries to keep us supplied with craft beer, so you can take your pick. In fact, why don't you and your handsome boyfriend come to the Grand Opening tomorrow night? Everything is on the house for my special guests."

"Sounds like fun! Welcome to Crested Peaks, Alice. We're thrilled you're here!" I head back to Marcall's relieved that our new neighbor seems like she'll fit right in. It's taken so long to get a tenant in place we were beginning to wonder if it would ever happen.

Considering the reason it was open in the first place, was the previous tenant was stabbed to death in the kitchen. We were worried that Rita, the poor landlord, may never rent it.

Once Damien returns from the store, and I make sure I fill him in on every detail of Alice's visit, as well as invite him to the grand opening tomorrow, we decide to close a little early today.

It's been a quiet afternoon and such a gorgeous spring day; I decide to go for a walk instead of heading straight home. As I stroll along Main Street, I pause to enjoy all the flowers and trees bursting with blooms.

Shop keepers are out and about greeting people, and many of them are displaying extra decorations and flowers. Everybody is in an especially good mood now that the snow is melting, and we can all be outside more.

I'm grateful for this gorgeous day and that I live in such a beautiful town. The mountain peaks surround us, and even though I see them every day, I'm still in awe every time I stare at their miraculous beauty.

They're still topped with leftover spring snow this time of year, but the aspen trees are budding with green leaves while the wildflowers burst forth in a multitude of colors.

I'm so busy admiring Mother Nature's paint pallet that I run headlong into a man who apparently hasn't stopped to smell the roses. "Watch where you're going lady!" he snarls.

"I'm so sorry! Are you okay?"

"I'm fine. How about a little less daydreaming and a little more awareness of where you're walking? You don't own the sidewalk."

"Again, I'm terribly sorry."

He glares at me one more time and stomps off with a huff. Well! Excuse me! It's not like I ran into him on purpose. Or that I didn't apologize. Sour puss.

Fortunately, it's rare to come across someone like that in Crested Peaks. The town is usually bustling with low key tourists enjoying the experience, or with locals who are already used to the laid-back atmosphere.

Not only does this guy's personality stick out like a sore thumb, so does his appearance. His expensive tailored suit and perfectly quaffed hairdo give him away as a non-local. Oh well. I glare back at him as I continue on my way. I refuse to let someone like that ruin my walk.

When I find myself in front of the library, I wonder if Miles is in. Ever since Miranda told me about the Colorado mountains hiding a treasure trove of rare gems, I've been curious to learn more.

Sure, some might argue that once again I'm investigating a crime that's best left to the police and the FBI. But what if, on the off chance, organized crime has come to our picturesque mountain town to cause trouble?

Shouldn't Drew know more about this? Besides, it's not like I'm investigating an actual person. Just looking more into a particular topic. And yes, in case you were wondering, I'm a master at justifying certain things.

Besides, one could argue that I'm just interested in learning more about Colorado and its history. Diamonds are interesting, after all. And it could be fun to learn more about what's buried deep in these glorious peaks.

By the time I reach the front door I've almost convinced myself this is pure curiosity and nothing more. And maybe I'll even check out a book while I'm here.

I tiptoe along the plush carpet and down the hallway in the direction the desk clerk shows me. Miles is in his office, with the door open, so I gently tap on the frame. He breaks into a surprised smile when he sees me. "Hey, Charlotte! What a nice surprise! Come on in! What brings you by the library today?" he asks, motioning to a chair in front of his desk.

"I started this as just a walk, but when I ended up here, I thought I'd pop in to say hello."

"I'm glad you did. It's been a second since I last saw you. I admit I didn't get out much this winter. I mostly stayed home and read."

"It's a bit of a catch-22 isn't it? We live in the mountains, where much of our income depends on the skiers, which then depends on how much it snows! But then it's tough sometimes just to get out your own front door."

"Yeah," he sighs. "And as much as I hate to close the library during a blizzard, I do love to sit home and read." He snaps his fingers. "What I need is a day where I'm snowed in at the library instead of at home. How great would that be!"

As much as I love his passion and enthusiasm; I'm biting my lip to keep from laughing at the idea of being excited about being stranded in a library. Although I guess as long as there were plenty of snacks and maybe a hidden bottle of wine, it certainly wouldn't be the worst place to be stranded.

He tsks, "You're trying not to laugh at me, aren't you?" I nod my head. Busted. "This isn't just a job for me Char. Books and learning are my passion. There are so many stories here. And facts and figures and art and everything!"

"Miles, I love that you love your job. And I see why Miranda likes you so much. You're a really stand-up guy, you know." And I also love the way his cheeks turn pink at the compliment, but I won't point that out. I think I've done enough damage to the poor guy for one day.

"And I know that it's meant a lot to Miranda to have you back in Crested Peaks. Even if you two kind of have a habit of, maybe, uh, getting involved, in, er, things you maybe, uh shouldn't?"

I tilt my head at him and narrow my eyes while he shifts uncomfortably under the scrutiny. "Gosh, Miles, it sounds like you've been talking to Detective Bailey recently." He starts to say no so I stare at him even harder. Fortunately, for Miranda's sake, this guy makes the worse liar.

"Okay, I have. He hoped that I could be a better influence on Miranda. Maybe encourage her to tell you no, when it comes to investigating any more crimes. Especially with the latest murder in Snowball Park."

I slump back in the chair and cross my arms over my chest. "And how did you respond to that?"

Now his cheeks are really pink. "I told him when Miranda gets an idea in her head, it's next to impossible to tell her anything, and I'm pretty sure you're the same way. And I'd really prefer not to be in the middle of all that."

He pushes up his glasses and finds a fascinating spot on the floor to fixate on. Now I feel bad. I didn't mean to scare him. I lean forward in my chair as I place a reassuring hand on his forearm. "Yes. Miranda and I are both very strong willed, and something tells me that neither you nor Detective Bailey would have us any other way. Still, you don't have anything to worry about because I am done with being a private investigator. I'm quite happy running Marcall's, thank you very much."

He breathes a sigh of relief, "I'm really glad to hear that."

"Hey, did Miranda tell you that the new restaurant next door to Marcall's is called Alice's Tavern and that they've already moved in?"

"No, she didn't. I wonder why?"

"She probably didn't have a chance to yet. I just found out myself this morning. Their grand opening is tomorrow night. You guys should come!"

"That sounds like so much fun. And perfect timing too! I think we all need a party. It seems like winter went on forever this year."

"It looks like the grand opening could be one of the biggest events this town has seen in a long time. And I'm excited to finally have a new tenant next door! It's been empty for so long I was beginning to think Rita was never going to fill the space."

"Alice's Tavern sounds like they'll have burgers and beer?" he surmises.

Knowing that Miles is a particularly dedicated craft beer aficionado, I tell him that Alice has already promised some of the best beer around. Which pleases him immensely. Now, if I could only figure out a way to ask about the diamonds without sounding like that's all I came here to do. He's obviously already on alert, over my penchant for solving mysteries, thanks to Drew. I don't want to make him any more suspicious for fear he'll tattle on me.

"You know, while I just happen to be here, I have a question you could probably help me with." Hopefully, that sounded casual enough. "Miranda mentioned you once told her that the Colorado mountains might have diamonds in them."

"Oh, yes, absolutely. Most people don't even realize it, but the only operating modern diamond mine in the entire US was in northern Colorado in the late 90s."

"1890s I assume?"

"No, the late 1990s."

"So just 25 years ago, they were mining for diamonds in Colorado? You've got to be joking."

"No ma'am. I told you most people don't even know that."

"Are they still mining there?"

"Nope, the mine shut down around 2000."

"Does the US have a lot of places with diamonds? I always just assumed people found them in South Africa, but that's about it."

"There was an area in Arkansas that had a mine operating in the early 1900s, but otherwise no."

"So, it's kind of amazing that they found diamonds in Colorado." Dating Miles must be a nonstop stream of information. No wonder Miranda finds him so fascinating. And hot too.

I have to admit, he's got this hot nerd thing going with his round glasses and sandy blonde hair that always seems just woke up messy. She said he's always trying to tame it, but it never quite does what he wants it to. If it were me, I'd just leave it messy.

"Of course, it's amazing!" he tells me.

"Is that the only place they've found diamonds, or have they located them anywhere else in Colorado?"

Miles looks at me suspiciously, and I'm worried the jig is up. He's going to think I'm too interested in all of this and squeal to Drew. "I have to ask, why the interest in Colorado diamonds? Have you always been this fascinated with our natural gemstones or has something happened recently?"

I plop both my elbows on his desk while resting my chin in my hands, in the hopes that this will make me look extra fascinated by what he's telling me. Miles may be a bad liar, but I was raised by a pair of con-artists so lying is in my DNA. "Ever since I moved back to Colorado, I've been eager to learn more about its history. I think it's important, you know?"

I must have convinced Miles of my sincerity because he runs his hands through his messy hair while deep in thought. I admit it, I feel a little bad for laying it on so thick, but this could be really important.

Once again, the integrity of Crested Peaks way of life may be at stake. "It's funny you ask that. It's been rumored for over a century that there are diamond producing volcanic pipes in some of the mountain regions, and one of them isn't far from here."

"You don't say!" I admit it, I'm a horrible person for manipulating Miles like this.

"It's called Gulver's Peak. But no one, that we know of, has ever been lucky enough to actually find any of them. There are even stories dating back to the Colorado Gold Rush that some of them found diamonds and didn't tell anyone." Then he breathes deep like it's almost just too much drama for him. "Or perhaps they just thought they knew where the diamonds were but died trying to get to them. Who knows what the real story is." He ends with a shoulder shrug.

My mouth drops into a surprised O. "So, we could be this close--" I hold my fingers up to indicate a tiny amount. "--to unmined diamonds right this very moment?"

Miles eyes are like saucers. "Yes!"

"That's incredible to think about."

"We have a great book here that you can check out if you want. It has tons of information on the different gemstones and minerals we have in Colorado. It even tells you where you could expect to find them. I mean if you were able to get there. There are several chapters devoted to Gulver's Peak alone." He chuckles. "It's a popular book, but I can see if it's in right now."

"Okay!" Even I have to admit, I really don't think the mafia is here for diamonds. I mean it still seems so far-fetched and too James Bond for our quaint little town, but it wouldn't hurt just to look into it a tiny bit, right? This way I can put my fears to rest and maybe learn something new while I'm at it.

Miles checks the database on his computer. "Okay, great, it's here, so I'll take you to it." He leads me through a winding maze of bookshelves which brings me back to my childhood where I spent many an afternoon devouring books.

I marvel at the number of books and the authors who sat in front of a typewriter, or a computer monitor, and took the time to write down words, one after the other, until it made an entire book.

I breathe deep, enjoying the smell of ink and paper. And then I sneeze. Several people look up from their books to glare at me for disturbing the peace. While I sometimes miss the experience of spending time in a library, I do enjoy being able to download a book instantly to my e-reader. There's no dust in that. Just some dirty fingerprints and maybe a bit of spilled wine now and then.

When we get to the spot where the book should be, Miles bends down and frowns.

"Is anything wrong?" I ask, noticing the scowl on his face.

He props his chin against his hand as he scans the shelf. "It's supposed to be here, and it should be in this exact spot," he explains, pointing to an open space left by the book's absence.

"Did someone return it to the wrong spot?"

"That's what I'm trying to figure out." He grimaces as he expands his search to nearby shelves. "Unfortunately, I don't see it anywhere around here. Somebody may have used it as a reference and then didn't put it back where it belongs. It really bugs me when they do that by the way!"

"It's okay, if you happen to come across it though, you can just let me know."

"I'll flag it in the system so if someone spots it, they'll know to save it up front for you, okay?"

"That's awesome. Thanks Miles. See you tomorrow night at the opening for Alice's Tavern."

I head back to Marcall's bookless, collect my familiars and the cat, and start to leave. But just as I'm turning out the lights, Miranda pokes her head in the door. "Hey, you want to work on some magic tonight?"

"Yes, please!"

"I'll be over at 7."

"Okay, see you then."

After nearly 20 years of pretending I wasn't a witch, thanks to my lawbreaking parents, my skills are lacking, to say the least, and there are a lot of things I don't know. My Gran tried to encourage me as a teen, but after what I'd been through with my parents, I refused, and she didn't push it.

For the longest time I thought if I pretended I wasn't a witch then I wouldn't become a felon like them. Since returning to Crested Peaks though, I've come to realize my parents were just criminals and it had nothing to do with them being Supernaturals.

Gran had the wisdom to realize that someday if I decided to practice witchcraft, I'd find a way to learn. I feel guilty for not taking advantage of her talent when I had the chance, but Miranda has been a very good teacher so far.

I assist two rabbits and one cat into the passenger seat while they regale me with stories of how their day went. One rather gruesome tale includes the rabbits challenging Stumpy to see how many grasshoppers he could catch and then eat.

The story ends with him vomiting up several grasshopper legs while the rabbits laugh themselves silly. And to think, I used to wish they could talk to me and not just my Gran.

Chapter 7

At precisely 7 PM, Miranda shows up brimming with ideas about what she wants me to work on next. One of the things she wants me to work on is the ability to repel objects by turning them around and forcing them to go in the opposite direction. Incredibly helpful, but also crazy difficult depending on what I'm trying to turn around.

When a deranged murderer held me at gunpoint in the Marcall's kitchen last year, I caught him off guard by flinging bakeware at his head. I bashed him hard too. Broke his nose and gave him a concussion.

When it was all over and I was safe, Damien complained that I ruined one of his best pans by leaving a huge dent in it. If only I'd had the ability to pick out his least favorite pans to pelt at the killer!

What we're working on tonight is much more complex. It pretty much defies physics. You know what I'm talking about. The concept of an object in motion tends to remain in motion, but we're not just stopping it, we're then sending it back to where it came from.

But witchcraft by its nature often defies the laws of physics, so here we are. I think about how I wish Drew could do this, just in case he's ever shot at. But as Miranda tells me, stopping something like a bullet is highly advanced magic. And it's not as easy as they lead us to believe in the books and movies.

We start with a pillow, so when I mess up, as Miranda assures me I'll do, it won't hurt. Hurt my pride, maybe but won't break anything. Although now that I think of it, I should probably put all the breakable things in the other room. Just in case.

Magic that's done on the fly, almost by instinct, requires intense concentration. It's one thing to open a locked door by focusing on it. It's entirely another to fully concentrate on something that's winging straight for my head.

The first time Miranda tosses the sofa pillow at me, I smack it away with my hand.

"That's not exactly what I had in mind," she lectures.

No kidding.

The second time she does it I duck. "If you aren't taking this serio usly..." she warns.

"I can't help it! It's instinct to move when something is speeding towards a person's head, you know!"

"Me barely tossing a pillow in your direction is hardly speeding. And you have to override your instincts by focusing on your powers! Let's try it again."

This time I force myself to concentrate on the pillow instead of ducking, and it hits me in the face.

"That's better!"

"Better for who?" I ask.

Then she throws another pillow and, once again, smacks me in the face. "You have to keep your eyes open!"

Crap. This is so much harder than I realized. I have to concentrate as hard as I can at the object ricocheting toward my head and keep my eyes open.

After about six times of getting smacked in the face with the pillow, I finally manage to stop it right before it hits me, and it drops to the ground. "There you go!" Miranda shouts.

"But I'm supposed to aim it in the opposite direction," I protest.

"At this point, I think you'd best just concentrate on stopping it. You need to walk before you can run."

Miranda throws the pillow at my head another dozen times. Each time, she throws it a bit harder, and each time I manage to stop it before it hits my head. On the 12th try it kind of sort of wobbles a bit in the air before it falls to the ground. I'm pretty sure I was this close to moving it in the opposite direction.

After nearly an hour of Miranda throwing pillows at me, each with increasing force, I'm easily stopping it before it gets to me. After awhile I can even reverse it somewhat, but not with as much force as she's using.

"That's okay. This is a tricky skill to master, and you're doing great so far. Let's do one last time and call it a night. Now really focus this time. Give it everything you've got."

I'm so ready for this practice session to be done, and to pour myself a glass of wine, that I hyper focus on the pillow the moment it leaves Miranda's hand. In fact, I'm so focused that I stop it mid-flight and send it straight back, hitting her in the face.

I'm elated and horrified at the same time. Miranda stumbles backward in surprise while the rabbits laugh uproariously. And if you've never heard a rabbit laugh, you're missing out.

"That was impressive, " Miranda says in a very measured tone. "And now you owe me a glass of wine." She looks over at the rabbits. "Is it just me or are they laughing?"

"They're laughing."

"Stinkers."

We settle down on the couch with some wine and a small fruit and cheese plate. A much-deserved reward if you ask me. "Drew working overtime on the murder these days?" Miranda asks

"I've barely seen him since it happened. They're working with the FBI, and it's all very secretive. I know they're extremely concerned about why organized crime has shown up here of all places."

"Miles mentioned that you stopped by the library today."

"He was very helpful. He says there's a book I should read. It's all about Colorado's gemstones. But it wasn't where it's supposed to be, so I guess I'll just have to wait on that."

"Do you really think it could have something to do with diamonds? Seems kind of far-fetched? Even though I'm the one who brought it up in the first place?" she laughs. "It was the only thing I could think of at the time."

"I guess, but it seems like anything can happen around here. After all, who knew that there was an entire underground tunnel system used for smuggling during the Gold Rush and that it led to my cafe?

"If organized crime is checking out our area, it would have to be for something huge, wouldn't it? Something they couldn't really get anywhere else. And according to what Miles said, I'm beginning to think it really could be diamonds."

"Wouldn't it be wild if it were true? Aside from the whole murder and organized crime thing of course. We could be sitting on diamonds and not even know it?"

At that, we both look down at my couch and then giggle. "I said almost the exact same thing to Miles!"

"And that's why we're best friends!" Miranda exclaims.

We spend another hour comparing customers who frequent both of our places and discussing the latest gossip from Gladys. We've been on high alert hoping for additional glimpses of the reality tv stars.

Miranda was also mad I didn't let her know right away about my sighting in the grocery store. We wonder if it would be possible to sneak up to Old Man Finley's place to see if we could catch them together. Especially if what Gladys told us is accurate.

Miranda finally stretches out her legs in front of her. "I guess I should be getting home now. The coffee world comes early these days."

"So does the breakfast world!"

Just as I see Miranda to the door, Drew shows up with a bouquet of fresh spring flowers. "Looks like I'm leaving just in time," Miranda says, tilting an eyebrow at me. "Don't worry Andrew, I was just leaving! You have your girl all to yourself now."

Drew smiles and nods his head. He looks exhausted. "These must be for me. Although the rabbits would like to eat them if given a chance."

"Uhhh no, they're for you. To look at. Not to eat."

"Thank you. That's very sweet of you. I'll get a vase for them."

"I feel bad that I haven't been around lately, but this case is just kicking all our butts."

"Any new leads?"

Drew slides his hand down his face and sighs in frustration. He looks defeated. "Our intelligence tells us that the mafia boss known as The Jackal is either headed here or is here already, and that's a really bad sign. It means that organized crime has a vested interest in Crested Peaks."

I'm running water into a vase for the flowers, so I'm sure I didn't hear Drew correctly. "The Jackal? Are you kidding?" I'd laugh if Drew didn't look so worried. "Do they all have nicknames? First, we have Bubblegum and now the boss who goes by Jackal?"

He shrugs as he flops down onto my couch, sighing loudly. "The worst part is we don't actually know who this guy is. There's no known picture of him on record. The FBI has come close to nabbing him before but not close enough to identify him. He's one of the most dangerous and wanted men in the world."

"But you still don't know exactly why Bubblegum showed up in the park dead or why organized crime is interested in Crested Peaks?"

"No, we don't know for sure. We obviously have leads that we're running down and several working theories, but not of them are solid."

"Would you like to hear my theory?"

"Sure!"

"Diamonds!"

"Diamonds?" For a second, he looks like he's about to laugh but then thinks better of it.

"Yes, it's the only thing that makes sense. I'm assuming that for organized crime to be setting up shop in Crested Peaks, we'd need to have something worth a lot of money. Otherwise why bother?"

"Go on."

"Miles was telling me--"

"--you told Miles?"

"No! But Miranda—"

"—you told Miranda."

"Well yeah, but you knew that would happen."

"I did."

I pause, waiting for him to say something more. When he doesn't, I continue with my theory.

"Miranda mentioned that Colorado mountains are full of unknown gemstones. Like, really valuable gemstones and minerals, and that Miles was the one who told her about that once. So, I asked him about it. He said we actually have diamonds buried in Colorado. And it's rumored there's an ancient volcano buried nearby in Gulver's Peak that contains unmined diamonds."

I look at him expectantly, waiting for him to be excited that I've blown his whole case wide open. Instead, he just stares back at me blankly.

"But what do you think of my theory?"

"Anything is a possibility. Although that's remote."

I pout.

"All we have so far is a dead mobster. We don't know who killed him. It's usually either one of their own, looking to move up in the hierarchy, or it's a rival crime family hoping to send a message. But in this case, we're still at a loss. We're investigating every possibility."

"So, you'll look into the diamond smuggling."

"When I get the chance, yes."

I decide it's probably best to leave it for now. When I investigated two murders, that I was accused of last year, it aggravated Drew in a huge way. I'll have to proceed carefully with this, or he'll shut me down completely.

I can't help it if sometimes he's just too overworked to see the entire picture. "Are you still up for going to the grand opening of Alice's Tavern tomorrow night?"

"Yes, I'm taking the night off no matter what!"

"I'm just so glad poor Rita finally got someone in there. I hated walking past it every day, looking all empty and forlorn. The empty restaurant was a constant reminder of Tony's death and my own close call. It will be nice to see it full of happy people again."

"I'm already hungry for onion rings," Drew says.

Drat. Now I'm craving onion rings.

Chapter 8

Morning seems to come quicker than usual. It's never a good idea to stay up late when you have to be alert and friendly before sunrise.

But after the lunch crowd files out, I take on the most unpleasant task of updating the inventory. I never realized how much paperwork is involved in running a restaurant. I keep telling myself I need an assistant. Perhaps I should take myself seriously and interview some people.

When I hear the door chime, I scurry to the front, but I'm stunned when I see who it is. It's the rude guy from the sidewalk yesterday.

"Is it too late to order?" he snaps when he sees the look of surprise on my face.

Well, hello to you too. "Of course not! What can I get for you?"

"I'm in the mood for pancakes."

I hand him a list of the various pancake specials we have for the day. "We have several types of pancakes, we even have a vegan ginger lemon pancake that's out of this world, or if there's something different you'd like--"

"--plain pancakes are fine," he interrupts

Why doesn't that surprise me? I let Damien know I need a stack of plain pancakes while I keep a watchful eye on the stranger. He's definitely not from around here. He's in another expensive suit, and he's carrying a briefcase. Who carries a briefcase anymore?

"What brings you to Crested Peaks?"

"Business."

"What kind of business?"

He looks annoyed, "Just business."

Okayyyy. I know the customer is always right, but this guy is really stretching it. I continue to watch him when Damien tells me the pancakes are up. I take them from the order window and place them, along with some silverware, in front of the Creepy Stranger as I've now decided to call him. "One order of fresh pancakes. What kind of syrup would you like? We have several different flavors or perhaps some fruit com--"

"--plain is fine."

Who eats pancakes without syrup? Now I really don't trust him.

When he opens his briefcase to pull out a file, I yip and immediately cover my mouth with my hand. There's a thick book on Colorado gemstones under the file. He stole it from the library!

What if he stole it because he didn't want anyone to know he was researching diamonds in the mountains? Oh crap, what do I do now? Just act cool. Pretend you didn't see anything.

Creepy Stranger catches me staring wide-eyed anyway and slams the briefcase shut. I'll just be cool until he leaves. But maybe I should call Drew and let him know there's a criminal eating plain pancakes at Marcall's right now. But if I call him, the mobster will hear me. I'll text him instead.

Me: Are you busy?

No, wait, that sounds weird. Are you busy? There's a mobster in the cafe.

Me: I need you to come over here asap.

No, wait, what if I'm wrong? I'll scare Drew to death, and then he'll be furious that I dragged him here on a wild goose chase. Think, Charlotte, think. What should I say?

Me: If you're not too busy right now, I think a mobster is eating plain pancakes at Marcall's.

Ugh. I don't know the protocol for alerting the police to a potential suspect. Why does this have to be so hard?

I slink into the kitchen, never taking my eyes off Creepy Stranger until I close the door.

"What are you doing?" Damien asks so abruptly he startles me.

"Shhhhh!" I scold him waving my hand in a downward motion.

"Why are we whispering?" he whispers back.

I shake my head and point out toward the dining area. Damien tries to peek through the order window, but I pull him down low.

"What is wrong with you?" he hisses.

"The guy eating the pancakes is part of a crime family."

"Are you kidding me?"

"No! Why would I joke about something like that?"

"Did you let Drew know?"

"No. Not yet."

"Why not?"

"Because I don't know for absolute certain he's in the mob. I'm just reasonably sure."

Damien gives me that look.

"If I call Drew down here and it turns out he's just a rude business-man from Denver, then he'll be mad at me because he's busy trying to track down the real mobsters."

"But what if you're right?"

"That's exactly what I'm saying! If I am right, we have to keep an eye on him."

Damien peers up through the window again. "He's gone."

"No!" I stand up to see that he has indeed left. "Rats! Good thing I got a picture." I snapped it with my phone when Creepy Stranger wasn't looking, so I can show it to Drew, and he can run it through their database, or whatever he usually does, and see who this guy really is.

Chapter 9

By the time we get to Alice's party I wonder if we'll be able to get a table, the whole place is jam packed. We love a good party in Crested Peaks. I can't believe how much Alice has changed.

When Tony was here, the tables were covered in starched white tablecloths, along with a single elegant lily and a small white candle on each. The plates were made of fine China with gold etching around the edges.

Every napkin was perfectly pressed and presented, and the flatware was so long and delicate I almost hated to dirty it. Not really my kind of thing, but the food was incredible.

Alice transformed the space into a much more casual and cozy gathering spot. I can picture us hanging out, sipping a beer, and enjoying a burger and fries on a Friday evening after work.

Where Tony's was clearly designed for a romantic dinner for two, Alice's has a ton of seats at the bar, along with numerous tables that have stools for seating groups of diners.

Maybe it's just the cover band rocking it in the background, the smell of beer and fries tickling my nose, or watching neighbors greeting each other after a long cold winter, but the longer I stand here, the more excited I get about our new neighbor. This is amazing!

When Alice sees us, she quickly threads her way through the crowd and manages to avoid spilling even a single drop of beer in the pint glass she's carrying. "Howdy again neighbor!"

"Hello Alice!" I shout over the music. "You have quite the party going here."

"Isn't it marvelous? I love Crested Peaks! And this must be your beau."

"Yes, this is Andrew. Andrew, this is Alice, Crested Peaks newest entrepreneur."

"I'm glad you decided to give our sleepy little town a chance. I know Rita has been eager to get a new tenant in here. It's been too long," Drew tells her.

"Yes, it's a shame what happened to the previous tenant and all. But Rita was happy to get a new one, and while she drives a hard bargain, she gave me a great deal on the place."

"Speaking of Rita," I continue to shout, "is she here? I haven't seen her in forever, and I want to congratulate her!"

Alice laughs as she scans the crowd. "She was the first one in the door, so I know she's here somewhere."

"Don't worry about it," I assure her. "I'm sure I'll see her at some point tonight."

"Jordan!" She snaps her fingers at a nearby waiter. "Get these folks a table and whatever they want, okay?"

Jordan scurries over. "Right this way, please," he says as he directs us to the nearest open spot.

"Can I get you started with a craft beer?"

"That would be great. What do you have in an IPA?" I love IPA's. The hoppier the better. Drew is a big sissy and can't handle them. He complains they're too bitter, so he always opts for a wheat beer.

"We have a triple dry hop from a brewery in Ft Collins I'm sure you'll like."

"I'll take it!"

"And for you, sir?"

Drew looks at me questioningly. "What do you have in a blonde ale?" I ask the waiter on Drew's behalf while trying really hard not to giggle.

"We have a seasonal spring ale with peach."

Now I'm biting my lip so hard to keep from laughing I'm surprised I don't hurt myself. "Oh, that's perfect," I tell the waiter as Drew rolls his eyes at me. Like it's my fault his girlfriend has to order beer for him.

After the waiter leaves to get our beer, I tell Drew. "I have something to show you."

"In public?" he asks. "That could be interesting."

I glare at him. "I'm trying to be serious here!"

He raises his hands in defeat. "All right, I apologize, what's up?"

"I'm pretty sure I've seen a member of the Calazzo crime family around town and he came into the café today and had pancakes. Plain pancakes I might add. With no syrup. Who does that? I think he's The Jackal!"

From the look on Drew's face, I think I should have left out the rant about the pancakes.

"I even got a picture of him. He just looks creepy, don't you think?"

"Charlotte, I already warned you not to get involved in this."

"I did not go out looking for this. He came into the café all on his own." I show Drew the picture I took earlier. It's a little blurry, but you can still mostly make out the guy's face.

"I have no idea who that guy is."

"Can't you just run him through your crime database or whatever and see what turns up?"

"On what grounds?" Drew asks as he looks around, worried someone might hear us discussing this. "We don't just investigate people based on their pancake preference and the fact you think he 'looks creepy.'"

"It's not just that! There's a book in the library on Colorado gemstones that Miles was going to give me to read, but it was missing. When the Creepy Stranger opened his briefcase at the café, I saw it in there. He must have stolen it from the library because the mob wants to smuggle diamonds out of Colorado."

"You mean you saw a book you think resembles the one Miles suggested to you at the library. And you're obviously investigating this since you're talking to Miles about those kinds of books. Even though, again, I've told you to stay away from this and let the CPPD and the FBI handle it."

Yikes. He's extra annoyed with me this time. "You have a successful café, good friends, and a superb boyfriend obviously. Throw in a pair of talking rabbits and their weird cat friend, and you have such a fulfilling life. Why, with all of that, must you continue to put yourself in the middle of dangerous situations?"

"I don't think I put myself in the middle of these things. I keep telling you, they find me!"

"I will make you a deal. If I learn that your diamond smuggling theory has merit, I will let you know, okay? That still doesn't mean you can help with the investigation. But if for some bizarre reason I learn that the mob is here to smuggle diamonds, you'll be the first person I tell—"

I start to raise my finger to interject and make a point.

"—but unless and until that time comes, I still expect you to stay far away from this investigation. Got it?"

"I suppose," I grumble.

"Now let's just enjoy this rare night out, okay? I see that Tom and Damien just showed up with their dog."

I turn around to see them waving at us from the porch. They've brought Bubbles, so they're sitting outside. Bubbles looks very happy with all the attention she's getting from the party-goers.

The rabbits have never met her, but I wonder if she'd talk to them like Stumpy does. Although even if she did, I probably wouldn't tell Damien. Talking rabbits already make him nervous. I can only imagine what he'd do if his own dog could talk.

"Hey, you two!" Miranda announces, taking us by surprise.

"You made it! See if they can rustle up two more chairs, and you can sit with us," I tell her.

"Oh, that's okay. I think we're going to grab a seat at the bar," Miranda responds. "One of the brewers is personally tapping his own keg pretty soon, and Miles is hoping to talk to him."

"Just so you know, Charlotte," Miles begins, "I'm still looking for the book you wanted, but I can't seem to find it anywhere."

Of course, I can't help but look triumphantly at Drew. The book isn't in the library anymore, it's in the hands of the mob. Drew responds to my look by giving me a salty one of his own.

"Uh oh, did I get in the middle of something?" Miles asks.

"Charlotte here is convinced that the mafia wants to secretly mine for diamonds in Gulver's Creek, and they desperately need your library book to figure out how to find the diamonds."

Now it's my turn to return Drew's salty look. He didn't have to say it like that. Telling it like that makes it sound ridiculous. It's not like he has a better theory.

Miles looks taken aback by this, and now I feel extra bad about pestering him yesterday. "I thought you said you were just interested in Colorado history."

"I am, it's just that Miranda mentioned--"

"--oh, hey, check it out, there's two seats open at the bar now. If we don't grab them this second, they'll be gone." Miranda says as she pulls Miles toward the bar and away from the awkward silence that's suddenly descended on our table.

"Seriously Charlotte? You two dragged Miles into this?"

"To be fair, Miranda just mentioned it in passing. I'm the one who accidentally on purpose ended up at the library." I confess, sighing loudly.

Thankfully, a much-needed distraction finally arrives in the form of our food order. Drew dives right into his burger and onion rings while I tackle a towering quesadilla made with pinto beans and green chilies drizzled with beer cheese sauce. It sounded so unique I just had to try it.

After about the third bite, Drew moans, "Don't tell Damien, but this is fabulous."

"I was just thinking the same thing," I admit. I always have to be careful when describing food that wasn't cooked by Damien. I suspect he'll be especially touchy when it comes from next door.

"The official response will be 'it's okay' yes?" Drew asks.

"That's usually the safest route," I concur.

"I already know the guys are going to want to take up a regular table here every Friday afternoon."

"I was thinking the same thing earlier," I tell him, nodding my head. "How fun would it be to stop in here after work for dinner and a beer, right?" We continue stuffing our faces with Alice's fabulous food while carefully avoiding uncomfortable topics like diamond smuggling and the mob.

Drew finishes off his beer and tosses his napkin onto the table, and grins. "As much as I would love to continue the happier parts of this evening, I need to get back to work."

"Yeah, I don't want to be up late again tonight. I've been dragging all day."

On our way out we wave to Miranda. Miles doesn't see a thing because he's involved in a serious discussion with a brewer. Alice is surrounded by a crowd of customers who look like they love the new place so I just give her a wave too.

And aside from Drew thinking my theories about diamond smuggling and Creepy Stranger being The Jackal are way off, dinner was great. I think Alice's Tavern will be a huge success, and it will be a blast having her next door.

We stop at the patio to greet Tom and Damien and Bubbles. She gets her own Pupizza. A pup sized personal pizza that she eats in about 3 bites. She's one of those dogs who always looks like she's smiling and today she's wearing a pink bow on her collar.

Damien starts to bring up the Creepy Stranger, but I give him a look that halts him in his tracks. I don't need another lecture from Drew about how we need to mind our own business.

Drew heads back to the station to continue working. I think he's more worried than he's letting on about all of this. If only he would let me help him.

It's not like I'm trying to chase down the bad guys with a gun or anything. I'm just quietly investigating in the background while leaving the dangerous stuff to him.

I arrive home to two glaring rabbits. "Stumpy says you smell like a dog," Marshall informs me.

"That's because I saw Bubbles tonight."

"He says dogs smell weird," Marcus chimes in.

"Tell Stumpy I said thank you, and I'll take that under advisement."

"He says you're welcome."

Somehow, I ended up with three talking animals under one roof. How did I get so lucky? When I was little, I often thought my grandma was just pulling my leg when she claimed to be talking to the rabbits. I wished that I could talk to animals, but I knew Gran was rather eccentric, so I thought it might all be just stories.

And now here I am having what are often bizarre conversations w the rabbits and their friend. And yes, some of what they've told me has been invaluable. After all, no one thinks to hold back while talking in front of animals. It's not like they can repeat what you say, right?

Chapter 10

The next day when Miranda stops at Marcall's I fill her in on Creepy Stranger and how I'm sure he has a stolen library book in his briefcase.

"Ohhhh Miles won't like that. He gets outraged when people try to steal books."

"Don't they have some kind of security tag on them?"

She laughs. "In Crested Peaks? No. Theft isn't a huge problem for the library here. Especially when you can buy a lot of books these days for a few dollars at most and have it delivered to your doorstep. Stealing them isn't worth it."

"So, it would be easy to steal, especially if you were a dangerous mobster who doesn't want anybody knowing that you have that book!"

"Do you still have the picture of Creepy Stranger?" Miranda asks as I watch a lightbulb go on over her head.

"Of course!"

"What if he's staying at the Hotel Glacier? The chances are good, right?"

"We can ask Harvey if he's seen him." I shout back to the kitchen, "Hey Damien, we're going out for a bit."

"Okay, not looking for dead bodies I hope?" he shouts back.

"Not this time!" I tell him.

Miranda and I hurry toward the Hotel Glacier. It's the town's most prominent hotel which, like many of the buildings around here, dates back to the mid and late 1800s. In its heyday, it was pure opulence. Where the rich and famous stayed. Now its main draw is its history, ghost stories, and paranormal activity.

Harvey, one of the hotel's most well-known spirits, likes to wax poetic about the good old days. He loves to remind us that the hotel was considered an architectural miracle at the time; considering the materials they needed to build it were carried by covered wagons over treacherous mountain passes. It was even the first in the area to have actual gas lights inside the building. No expense was spared.

Some ghosts still live there. A few of them are like Harvey and interact with guests, while some lurk in the shadows and torment the guests. Still, others are likely just urban legends. But there are always tales of noises in the middle of the night. Things being moved when no one is around. Gusts of icy air blowing through rooms, even when the windows are closed.

They get a lot of tourists who stay there just for the experience. Halloween is their biggest holiday of the year, where they host a huge bash. Harvey ran the Hotel Glacier when it first opened but was caught in the middle of a shootout between the sheriff and a bank robber.

His spirit simply stuck around to help with the daily duties of the hotel. He's also been known to run off customers he doesn't like. Similar to Gladys, Harvey often has the tea on who's doing what within the town. Although unlike Gladys he's limited to staying on the hotel grounds and can get a little grumpy when he thinks he's being used just for information.

Once we get there, it takes a while to locate him. You can't just page a ghost after all. Well, you can, but he'd just ignore it anyway. We have to be patient.

Standing around in the lobby and loudly talking about how we desperately need his expertise often helps. He eventually pops up out of nowhere to see what we want.

"Ladies! Long time no see."

"Hello Harvey!" we chorus.

"It sounds like you need my help."

"We do," I explain as I start to hold up the phone to show him Creepy Stranger's photo.

"So that's the only time you bother to come and see me, when you need something?" Harvey sounds particularly grumpy today. Who knew ghosts could get grumpy? "I can't move around town like the rest of you. No, I'm stuck here waiting for people to come to me. And everybody always wants something. Question after question. Where's this? Where's that? How do I get here? How do I get there? It's exhausting."

"I'm really sorry about that Harvey, it's just that we've been so busy with everything that's going on lately..." I start to show him the picture again, but he continues to complain.

"Oh sure, you're busy, you're all busy, you all have lives. Meanwhile, I'm stuck here with nothing better to do than explain things to people and give them directions."

"I swear from now on we'll make it a point to come to visit you even when we don't need anything." Miranda promises.

"I'm going to hold you to that missy!" Harvey shakes his finger at us.

"So, if you could just look at--"

"I don't mind telling you that I have been harassed by some of the most disagreeable types recently. New people I've never seen before. People who aren't the usual tourists."

Miranda and I look at each other. "What do they want to know?" she asks.

"It's interesting that you should ask," Harvey pauses to make sure we're hanging on to every word. He has a flair for the dramatic. I guess I would too if I were a ghost. What else would there be to do?

"One of the men who was quite rude to me was the same man who died in the park."

"Are you sure?" I ask.

"Well of course I'm sure. I saw his picture in the paper."

"And he was here asking questions before he died?"

"Yes, he and his friend asked me if it was possible to rent a helicopter. They were so rude. I just don't understand it. People have no manners these days. Back in my day--"

"--what did you tell them about the helicopter?" I interrupt, hoping he doesn't get short with me for being rude, but this could go on forever.

"I sent them to Harry's Helicopter Rides."

This isn't the first time we've dealt with Harry, the helicopter pilot. Harry unknowingly flew a murderer back to Crested Peaks from Breckenridge last year, just so the murderer could maintain his alibi.

It wasn't Harry's fault; he had no idea he was transporting a killer. I doubt he'd appreciate getting mixed up in mob business now, though. And what would they need with a helicopter?

"Do you recognize this man?" I ask, finally getting the chance to show him the picture on my phone.

"I sure do. He was the dead guy's friend. He's staying here as a guest right now. I don't like him either. He even asked me where the library was. That was weird. Tourists don't ask about the library."

I knew it! Miranda and I turn to each other triumphantly. He stole that book from the library.

"I've noticed him with another man quite a bit too. A disagreeable lot if you ask me." He shudders. At least, I think it was a shudder. I'm not sure ghosts actually do that.

"Do you know either of their names?"

"Nope, I don't pay attention to that. It's not like I work at the front desk anymore."

"Okay, thank you, Harvey, you've been very helpful. But we have to get back to our shops."

"Wait, seriously? You're leaving already? See what I mean? No one wants to hang out with a ghost. You all just use me."

"I swear, we'll be back soon just to say hello, and we'll stick around and talk, okay?"

"Yeah, yeah, yeah," he grumbles, disappearing with a pop while we dash out the front door and back to Marcall's.

We're so excited we practically sprint the entire way back. "I knew it Miranda, I just knew it. Creepy Stranger stole that book from the library, and more than ever I think he's The Jackal. One of the most wanted criminals of all time was in my café eating pancakes yesterday. Plain pancakes, I might add."

Miranda is confused. "Who's The Jackal, and why was he eating pancakes at Marcalls? And who eats plain pancakes?"

Uh oh. I probably wasn't supposed to say that. Drew knows that I tell Damien and Miranda everything, but this is serious. Like FBI most wanted murderer serious. But we've come this far together, so I might as well tell her the rest.

"There's a famous mafia boss known only as The Jackal. They don't know his real name, and no one actually knows who he is. But Drew says he's either headed to Crested Peaks or is here already, and I'm sure it's Creepy Stranger who stopped by for pancakes yesterday and who had the book he stole from the library in his briefcase."

"Well, don't tell Miles. He'll hunt him down himself."

"So, what do we do now?" Miranda asks. "Should we call Drew or the FBI?"

"If we do that, he'll know I've been investigating this, and he has repeatedly told me to stay out. 'It's too dangerous,' he bellowed at me. Besides, I already mentioned this to him, and he brushed it off. He insisted I mind my own business and let the cops handle it."

Miranda stops in the middle of the sidewalk. "Do you think we should talk to Harry?"

She just gets me. "I do."

"But if you aren't going to call Drew first, I think we should take Damien with us. A safety in numbers thing, you know. What, what is it, why the face?"

"You know how cautious Damien is. He'll never agree to this. He'll insist we call Drew first."

"Damien might actually have a point. I'm not sure we should be messing with international criminals."

"Oh c'mon, we're not in any danger where Harry is concerned. The only thing we'll do is ask him if Creepy Stranger has been there and what did he want. That's hardly risky. If you don't want to come with me, I'll go by myself." I turn on my heel and march in the direction of Harry's place.

"Okay, wait! How about this? We ask Damien if he wants to come with us. If not, I'll still go with you," Miranda suggests.

"Okay, deal." I know Damien won't like this one bit, but if he thinks he's keeping us safe, maybe we can talk him into it.

We poke our heads in the door at Marcall's. "Hey, Damien," I call out. "You want to come with—"

"What are you up to now?" he says standing in the middle of Marcalls dining area, his arms crossed, a scowl etched on his face. "I'm not going to like this, am I?

"We're just following up on a lead by talking to Harry. That's all. I swear." I hold my hand in the air, ready to swear an oath.

Damien looks confused. "Harry? As in Harry's Helicopters?"

I nod my head.

"Do I want to know why?"

"Harvey said that Creepy Stranger and the mobster who died in the park asked him where they could rent a helicopter," I explain as if this kind of thing just happened all the time and what would be unusual about running down leads from a ghost about a mobster. Okay, even I think I could be stretching this one.

Damien grabs my arms and pleads with me. "Charlotte, Drew has warned you over and over about these kinds of things. Just call him and let him check into it."

"I already told him what I think, and he basically dismissed it. We're not arresting anybody or chasing them down. It's not like I tackled Creepy Stranger yesterday and made a citizen's arrest. I'm just looking into it. I promise, if we come across something that looks dangerous, I'll call Drew right away."

He waggles a finger between the two of us. "I swear if you two get us in trouble or killed..."

"C'mon," I urge, "It's almost closing time, and the café is empty anyway. Let's just close up for the day and run over to Harry's for a moment."

Damien shakes his head slowly, "Fine. But don't say I didn't warn you."

I shout to the back and let the boys know we'll be out for a while. "Bring back some parsley!" Marshall shouts at me on my way out the door.

Chapter 11

Damien is unhappy that we went to Harvey looking for answers about Creepy Stranger. "You two aren't just going to get in trouble with Drew over this, you know. It could be dangerous."

"We're just asking questions," I reassure him. "It's not like I demanded to know the number of Creepy Stranger's room or anything."

Damien stops abruptly. "Are you kidding me? Harvey tells you that Creepy Stranger, who you think has mafia ties, is staying in the hotel. A hotel you just visited, and you still haven't told Drew?"

I resume walking, hoping Damien will decide to keep following us. "But what if we talk to Harry and he tells us that Creepy Stranger or Bubblegum Vinny just wanted a romantic helicopter ride with one of their girlfriends? Then Drew will be annoyed with me for wasting his time again."

"He's going to be especially annoyed if you end up dead because you're investigating organized crime when he specifically said you shouldn't."

"I promise you, right now, we're simply following up on a couple of innocent leads, that's all. Once I get more information, I'll take it to Drew."

"Did you tell him about The Jackal yet?" Miranda asks.

Damien stops in his tracks again. "What's a Jackal?"

I look to Miranda, "To be fair, we don't know for absolute certain that Creepy Stranger is The Jackal. I just happen to think he is."

Damien starts to head back in the opposite direction, muttering and cursing in Spanish as he does.

Miranda and I both jog after him and take an arm. "Drew says there's some super big-time mobster known as The Jackal who's headed to Crested Peaks," I tell him. "But we're not supposed to share that with anyone."

"And I may have made pancakes for him." Damien reminds us. "We're all gonna die," he sighs.

"We're not going to die!" I scold him as we gently lead him back in the direction we want to go. "We already know Harry personally because of everything that went down last year, so it's not a big stretch that we would stop by here for a brief chat. You know, just among friends."

***

"Did Detective Bailey send you?" Harry asks, relief crossing his face when he sees us walk in the door. Poor Harry. When he agreed to fly Bryce, the former business partner to my now-landlord's murdered husband, he had no idea he was helping him get away with murder.

I'm sure it was traumatizing, but it's odd that he's wondering if Drew sent us. "Why would Detective Bailey send us here?" I ask him.

"I left a message for him at the front desk of the police station this morning. I realized that the guy who was killed in the park, was the same guy who showed up here earlier this week asking me to fly him and a couple of friends to Gulver's Peak."

It's all I can do to keep from shouting a loud war whoop because I was right. Instead, I turn around and stare at Damien and Miranda, my eyebrows raised. "Did he say why?" I ask as I turn back slowly to face Harry.

He looks uncomfortable. "Should I wait to talk to Detective Bailey about this? Since he's the police and you're just...um...well... not the police?"

"You can tell us, and we'll pass it on to Detective Bailey," I explain as Damien makes worrisome noises behind me, and I signal him behind my back to hush. I know I've just crossed way over the line, but now that we're here, I can't help myself.

We're on the verge of blowing this thing wide open, I can just feel it, and I swear if Damien messes this up because he's nervous about what Drew might do, I'll never forgive him.

Besides, I'm not really lying or anything. I realize we're not actually here on behalf of Drew, but because I have immediate access to him, of course, I'll pass on any pertinent information.

Although that means Drew will know right away that I've been investigating, but we'll just cross that bridge when we come to it. I believe I've mentioned my ability to justify things in incredibly creative ways before, haven't I?

"I guess that would be okay." He looks skeptical but continues. For just a moment I feel a twinge of guilt for misleading him, but this is important after all. "They didn't explain why exactly, but the fella

who showed up dead in Snowball Park, and his two friends, said they
needed to transport some heavy equipment up to the peak, and would
I be able to do that? I immediately thought it sounded suspicious, but
I was willing to hear him out. Then, when he showed me what they
were offering me, I knew something was up for sure."

"What did they offer you?"

"He had a roll of bills. $10,000. Cash. Per trip."

"$10,000! Is that what people normally pay you?"

"Oh, heavens no," Harry says, laughing. "Not even close. And definitely not in cash like that. That's when I knew they must be up to
no good. I told them I'd have to free up some room on my schedule
and that I'd get back to them later. Honestly, I was just hoping they'd
give up and find someone else. When I saw the picture of the dead guy
in the newspaper, I decided I should let the police know."

"Can you tell me if this was the other guy?" I ask as I hold the phone
up.

"Yes. That's him. I was right, wasn't I? Those guys are no good."
Before I can ask anything more, his phone rings. "If you'll excuse me
for just a second. It might be my next tour calling. They're late."

"Sure, of course," I tell him.

The three of us put our heads together, whispering about what we
should do next.

"Why yes, Detective Bailey, thanks for returning my call."

Uh oh.

"I was just explaining everything I know to your friends. They said
they'd be happy to fill you in." There's a long, uncomfortable pause as
I attempt to swallow a large lump of awkward. Harry looks up at me
as his brows knit together with concern. "Of course, I'll put her right
on."

He holds the phone out to me. "Detective Bailey would like to speak with you."

Oh, dear. I gingerly take the phone from Harry as if I'm expecting it to bite me. Which, it actually might. "Hey Drew!" I offer with a completely false sense of bravado.

"Marcall's. Now."

Chapter 12

"I take full responsibility. I talked these two into coming with me even though they both urged me to call you first," I explain.

"I don't doubt that," Drew says as he paces around Marcall's lecturing us. "What were you thinking, running off like that on your own? These guys are wanted killers. As in professional killers. They chop people to bits and throw them in the ocean, never to be heard from again. You can't keep trying to solve this crime on your own."

"Now, to be fair," I point out, holding up my hand to emphasize my point. "I came to you with my theory about The Jackal and diamond smuggling, and you dismissed it."

"And I still do! We don't have enough evidence to assume that this Creepy Stranger guy you keep mentioning is The Jackal. We don't even know if The Jackal is in Crested Peaks yet."

"But Harvey said he saw the two of them together several times."

"And that's when you should have called me immediately and told me. Even if you thought I wouldn't believe you. But you didn't because you knew I'd be mad that you purposely went over to the hotel to discuss the situation with Harvey. A ghost.

"And what am I supposed to tell my boss about that anyway? 'Hey captain, my girlfriend, who is not a cop, has been investigating the organized crime case, even though I specifically told her not to. She talked to a ghost at the hotel, and he told her he saw these guys together, so lucky us, she's practically solved the case.' He'd laugh me out of the room. And I'd be lucky if that's all he did!"

"So maybe it's a good thing I didn't call you after all?" I offer. But Drew's death stare shuts down that theory. "But if we hadn't talked to Harvey, then we wouldn't have known to talk to Harry," I protest.

"Harry called me and left a message! He did the right thing! Then I obviously returned his call while you three were there playing amateur sleuth."

Oh yeah, I forgot about that part. Drew was irate, and I suppose with good reason. Or maybe some good reason. I just got so excited when Harvey acknowledged that he'd seen Bubblegum Vinny with Creepy Stranger. I knew they were connected somehow.

"Should we mention the part about Gulver's Peak?" Miranda leans over and mutters at me from behind her hand.

"What about Gulver's Peak?" Drew asks his agitation still clear.

I sigh, thinking it's just another thing he's going to dismiss. "Remember when I said I talked to Miles about the diamond mining, he specifically mentioned Gulver's Peak?"

"Yes."

"Harry said the mobsters wanted him to take them to Gulver's Peak."

"And you assume that makes your diamond smuggling theory correct?"

"I did at the time," I mumble.

"All right, look, it's certainly possible you're right." I look up at him hopefully. "But don't get too excited just yet," he warns me. "I'll meet with Harry at the station this evening so he can make a proper statement, and we'll discuss the possibility more then."

He continues to emphasize the word possible, but I'll take it. He's just been doing this job for so long he's a wee bit cynical. He can't imagine how anyone other than a highly trained police detective could solve a mystery. I consider reminding him how I helped solve the case last year but decide not to push my luck.

"I appreciate the fact that you three are obviously so committed to the well-being of this town. I truly do. But I worry about you. I worry about your safety, and I fear that you could inadvertently compromise this case.

"When we finally do figure out why organized crime is invested in Crested Peaks, we need to be able to shut them down. Okay? So please, I'm begging you, let the professionals handle this."

Damien and Miranda hang their heads like they're being scolded by their dad. "You're right Drew, I don't want to get in your way, and I definitely don't want to die anytime soon," Damien says.

He adds that last part for emphasis as he gives me a grumpy look. Although I don't blame them. I'm the one who keeps pushing this. Except it would be nice if they'd show at least a little loyalty to me.

"I'm with Damien. It's best that we let you guys handle this," Miranda chimes in.

Then the three of them turn to me, expectant looks on their faces. Et tu Brutus? "I apologize if I placed the two of you in danger at any point, and I don't want to mess up your investigation either, Drew. That's the last thing I want to do."

Drew narrows his eyes at me. I know he's waiting for me to swear I'll never investigate anything for as long as I live, but I don't want to lie point-blank to the guy. I mean, not right this second anyway. "Okay," he responds reluctantly, figuring that's probably the best he'll get right now. "I promise I will update you about the case as soon as I'm able, okay?"

The three of us nod our heads in agreement. I'm hoping he can get some useful information from Harry tonight at the station. I'd love to know more about what Bubblegum Vinny, Creepy Stranger, and the third guy told him.

What? I said I didn't want to mess up his investigation, and I mean it! Doesn't mean I'm not curious about what could happen.

That night Drew texts me.

Drew: Good news. Things went well with Harry, and he's working with a sketch artist to identify the third man from the group. Your Creepy Stranger shows up as an accountant from San Diego. However, given the company he's keeping, I doubt that he's just an ordinary accountant. And yes, signs point to you being right that he's involved with organized crime, so if he shows up at Marcall's again, you need to call me. BUT DON'T DO ANYTHING ELSE.

I knew it! **Me: So, he is The Jackal?**

Drew: I didn't say that. I just meant that we're seriously looking at him for being a mobster. We just don't know what level yet.

I'm still thinking Jackal, but whatevs. He'll just owe me when it turns out I'm right.

Drew: It's another long night for me, but I'll stop by Marcall's for breakfast tomorrow and fill you in on the details.

Me: Can't wait! Good night.

Drew: Good night. And please behave.

Me: You know me!

Drew: Yes, I do.

Party pooper!

Chapter 13

Every time the door chimes with a new customer, I look up anxiously. I want to know if the police department's sketch artist got anywhere with Harry and what it may have turned up.

Who knows, maybe the third guy is The Jackal. Except my money is still on Creepy Stranger. I notice Drew didn't tell me his real name. It's not like I'd cyber stalk him or anything and try to learn more about him.

After what seems like an eternity, Drew walks through the door. "He's here!" I hiss toward the back as Damien scurries through the kitchen door. The only other customers are a pair of teenagers in the corner playing some kind of video game on their phones, and I don't think they'd notice a bomb detonating in the middle of the restaurant.

I honestly feel bad for Drew. This case is wearing on him, and he looks more tired and worn out every time I see him.

"Damien Special?" Damien asks.

"Yes, please," Drew says, looking grateful. "And coffee!"

"Coming right up!" Damien races back to the kitchen so he doesn't have to miss a moment of the discussion.

"Did your sketch artist turn up anything new?" I know I should fuss over him more and ask him if there's anything I can do, but I'm dying to find out what he's learned since last night. I can play the doting girlfriend in a moment. Once he tells me something good. Besides, I have tried to help him, I just keep getting lectured about it.

"I'm sure you'll be highly interested to know that indeed, it appears the third man is none other than—"

"—The Jackal!" Damien exclaims as he comes out of the kitchen with Drew's burrito.

"No. And shhh!" Drew warns as he looks around the café to make sure no one is listening. "The third mystery man is a geologist from India - Dr. Aadiv Natt and he specializes in lost causes. He's well known for finding hidden veins of rare gemstones in, let's just say, unlikely places."

He looks like he's trying to swallow a ball of rubberbands; he's so uncomfortable. I, on the other hand, am trying really hard not to clap my hands with delight. I'm pretty sure I know where he's going with this.

He continues, "In light of this new evidence, we are seriously considering your diamond smuggling theory."

"So, what's next?" I'm eager to move this investigation forward. And it isn't even my investigation. Even though I might secretly think it is in my head.

Drew continues, "Harry has agreed to call them and arrange a meeting at his office this afternoon. He'll wear a wire, and hopefully, they admit to something we can arrest them on."

"This is so exciting!"

"I can't believe this is happening," Damien marvels. "You solved another case!"

"I know!" I shout.

Of course, Drew has to shut everything down with an icy stare. "We haven't solved anything yet. It's still just a working theory."

Damien opens his mouth to say something.

"And no, don't even ask if you can listen in."

Damien's mouth snaps shut as his face falls.

"Yes, I knew that was coming," Drew says.

Good thing Damien asked – or tried to – first because I was on the verge of asking the same thing.

"Don't look so disappointed, you two. After all, I came over here bright and early to share this with you when I shouldn't say anything in the first place, right? And I admitted that you may be on to something with your diamond smuggling."

Damien and I mumble in agreement. He's right. At least we got that. Although I'm still wondering if I can find a way to listen in on the conversation between Harry and the bad guys.

Everything is set. Harry is meeting with Creepy Stranger and the geologist this afternoon to discuss hiring him to transport them to Gulver's Peak. Drew and the FBI will be in a van nearby, listening to the conversation.

The second the bad guys admit they're planning to smuggle diamonds out of Colorado, bam! The good guys move in and capture them. Although Drew said, it's probably not that easy.

They'll need to openly admit that they're planning to drill on what's considered federally protected land and smuggle it out of Colorado. The bad guys aren't dumb, and it's kind of a long shot that they'll just admit that upfront to Harry.

***

As the clock inches ticks forward, I get antsy. "Hey Damien, I think I'll go for a walk around town. The weather's so nice after all. You can handle things here, right?"

"Charlotte, don't you dare."

"What, don't I dare go for a walk?"

"Please. I know what you're up to. You're going to sneak around Harry's area to see if you can catch any of the conversation. This is an official CPPD and FBI investigation. You can get in big trouble for interfering."

"Oh Damien, don't be such a spoilsport. I'm not interfering with anything. I'm just casually passing somewhat nearby and might be able to pick up some of the conversation. They wouldn't be this close to catching them if it weren't for me, you know."

"I get that, but seriously, this is big stuff. You can't just let me leave here. What if we get a last-minute rush?"

I look around the empty café. "We're like 10 minutes from closing. I'm pretty sure you can handle the stampede by yourself."

"I insist you stay right here," he calls after me. I feel kind of bad that poor Damien has to say that to my back as I walk out the door. But only kind of.

Harry's office is close to Snowball Park, so it's an easy walk to get there. He has a shop front where tourists stop in and reserve flights, but his helicopters are kept at a separate helipad closer to the airport, which is a little way out of town. Harry agreed to meet the bad guys at his office, which makes it easy for me to find a spot close by to listen in.

There's more than one van parked nearby, but I concentrate on each and determine that the blue one has three men inside it, so that must be it. I sneak into a tea shop directly across from Harry's office, order a tea, and tuck myself into the corner where I can see Harry and hear the men talking in the van. Have I mentioned lately how much I love being a witch?

The voices in the van are faint at first and a little fuzzy, but the harder I focus on them, the clearer they become. Obviously, I know which one is Drew's voice, but I don't recognize the other two at all, so I'm guessing they're FBI.

And then I hear Harry's voice. "Hey, you guys, can you hear me?"

"Yes, Harry, we're good. Remember, you can't keep talking to us. Just have a normal conversation when the suspects show up. You can't let on that someone else is listening." One of the FBI agents reminds him.

"Okay, yeah, right, of course. I keep forgetting. This is really weird," Harry stutters. Poor guy is obviously nervous. I would be too.

Drew's voice cuts in, "Just stick to the plan like we practiced. Let them do most of the talking. We need them to ask you to fly them to Gulver's Creek and for how much. We also need them to tell you what kind of equipment they want you to carry, because that will give us a better idea of what they're up to. Don't get creative or try to catch them in the act. That's for us to worry about. You just need them to hire you for the job, okay?"

"Okay, got it."

I gasp out loud when I see Creepy Stranger and the guy who must be the geologist approach Harry's office. This is real. And a little scary. I hope Harry can pull this off. I have the best view in the house if they get to bust these guys.

Harry stands up to greet them and wipes his hands on his pants before shaking hands with them. He must be sweating. I can't imagine what he's thinking right now. Facing down the guy who might be one of the deadliest criminals in the US and trying to act normal at the same time.

"We're really glad your schedule opened up," Creepy Stranger tells him.

I still can't believe he eats pancakes with no syrup. That's your first indication he's up to no good.

"Yeah, me too," Harry responds, his voice still a little shaky. "What was it you needed me to do again? By the way, where's your friend?"

"He's indisposed at the moment. No need to worry about him," the geologist points out.

"Of course, no worries." Harry wipes his hands on his pants again.

"This guy better not blow this," one of the agents in the van mutters.

"He'll be okay. He's got this," Drew responds.

"We want to get to Gulver's Peak, along with some equipment that we'll need for our expedition. We don't need you to stay or anything. We'll be camping up there for several days. We'll pay you half the amount we mentioned earlier and then half when you pick us up," Creepy Stranger explains.

"Yeah, we need to make sure you come back for us," the geologist chuckles. Yuck. These guys are just weird. Harry makes a halfhearted attempt to laugh, but it comes out more like a gurgle mixed with a choking noise, and they look at him strangely.

"We may need to make several trips if the first one is successful. Would you be interested in helping us with that?"

"Sure, sure, I could probably help with that. What exactly are you doing up there?"

"Uh oh," the FBI agent mutters.

"That's none of your concern," Creepy Stranger growls.

"Oh, yeah, I understand. I just thought if I knew what kind of equipment you'll be carrying and why you need me to take you there, I could be of more help," Harry laughs nervously.

One of the FBI agents swears inside the van. This doesn't seem to be going well. Instead of just waiting to let these guys talk, Harry tries to get everything out all at once. This could end very badly. And we still don't have them admitting to much of anything.

"We're willing to pay you a lot of money to just fly us up there. That doesn't include you needing to know why."

"Of course, no problem." Harry wipes his hands on his pants again. I bury my face in my hands. This is so bad.

"Why are you so nervous?" the geologist asks. "You're acting fishy all of a sudden."

"Who me? No, why do you ask?"

I sit up straight and on alert. It never occurred to me they could get suspicious and maybe even harm Harry. What if they shoot him? He could end up like Vinny!

When I hear Drew say, "All units be on alert, this is crashing fast. Move in on my mark." My heart races not only for Harry but for Drew and the other agents. Somebody could get hurt here. Or worse.

"I told you this was a bad idea!" the geologist scolds Creepy Stranger. "I said it seemed weird when he called us back. But oh no, you insisted we at least talk to him. He didn't act like this before, you know." The geologist turns back to Henry, "What are you playing at? Huh? Are you trying to shake us down for more money? Is that it?"

"No, uh, no, that's not it at all!" Harry stammers as he waves his hands in front of him. "I swear it isn't!"

"Then what is it?" the geologist barks as he advances on Harry. "What's going on here?"

I'm terrified for Harry but terrified for the police too. And without even thinking, as if I'm acting purely on instinct, I focus on the door to Harry's office, and I fling it open so hard the glass breaks.

"Hold your position!" Drew barks into the radio. "All units hold your position; it was just the wind!"

Meanwhile, Harry, Creepy Stranger, and the geologist all jump about a foot in the air when that happens. I hadn't meant to fling it open that hard. But it did the trick.

"What the hell was that?"

"It was just the wind man let's get out of here. We don't need this."

"You're lucky," the geologist sneers at Harry. "Thanks, but no thanks."

I breathe a huge sigh of relief when they march down the street and, Harry looks like he might cry right before he slumps to the floor. I hate that we're right back to where we started, but I'm grateful no one got hurt. We'll have to figure out another way to catch these guys.

I also feel bad about the broken door, but before I can do something to fix it, Drew and the FBI approach the office, and I have to duck down so Drew doesn't see me in the window. I'll make it up to Harry later somehow. Although saving his life was pretty good, but of course, he doesn't know that.

If Drew knew I was here, I'd never hear the end of it. I hide in the tea shop until they leave, and then I scramble back to Marcall's just in case Drew stops by. I'm going to have to play dumb when he tells me what happened. Goodness, this is getting complicated.

Chapter 14

When I arrive back at Marcall's, the door is locked, and the sign reads Closed. Phew. I'm hoping that means Damien has left for the day because I don't want to explain myself to him right now. He'll just say he told me so. Although I know if I don't at least text him to let him know I'm okay, I'll eventually find him on my doorstep demanding answers.

My entire body trembles while I concentrate on the lock. Open, I command, as the lock slides open. I then push open the door with shaking hands, but before I can close it behind me Alice is on my heels, and I yelp I'm so startled.

"Oh, my goodness, dear! I'm so sorry if I startled you! Are you okay? You look like you've seen a ghost. Although I guess in this town, it's certainly possible. She guides me to a chair so I can sit down, which I happily accept.

She thinks I'm shaking because she just startled me. Imagine if she knew that I nearly just saw a man killed. "You better sit down and let me get you a glass of water. I apologize for sneaking up on you like that."

"I'm okay, really, just didn't eat enough lunch today, I guess. I'm feeling a bit lightheaded."

"But you run a restaurant, sweetie!" She laughs such a deep earthy laugh I can't help but really like her.

"I know, the irony," I shrug. At least she seems to be buying my story. Still, she ventures back into the kitchen, where she rummages around for a glass to put some water in. Good thing Damien isn't here. He's very particular about who's allowed in his kitchen.

"Charlotte?" she calls up.

"Yes? Do you need some help?"

"No, but there are two rabbits back here staring at me."

"Oh, yes, they were my grandmas. That's Marshall and Marcus."

"They look like they're hanging on every word."

Because they probably are. "They're just weird like that."

She comes back into the dining area with a glass of water for me. "Did you know a two-footed cat was living next door when I signed the lease?"

"Yes, that's Stumpy. He lives with me now."

"Oh, I was just going to take him to the shelter." I swear I hear a growling noise from the kitchen.

"Eh, that's okay, he's no trouble, really." I bite my lip to keep from laughing at the urge to tell her the rabbits invited him to live with us. As much as I like her, and even though she knows I'm a witch, I don't need to tell everyone their story. There are actually very few people who know that part. And even fewer still who would believe it.

"I stopped by to see if you would be interested in a flyer swap." She hands me a stack of flyers advertising Alice's Tavern. "And of course, I'm happy to put your flyers out as well."

"Great idea!" I tell her as I get up to retrieve some Marcall's flyers under the counter.

"I'm so excited to be building a business and living here. I just love this town already!" she exclaims.

"I'm glad you're enjoying life in Crested Peaks. I lived here as a child but then left for a while. But I'm happy I came back."

"Your grandmother raised you for many years, right?"

"Yes, she did."

"Rita mentioned that too." She responds to my quizzical look. I'm beginning to think Rita talks a lot! She may give Gladys a run for her money.

She pats my hand. "If you're sure you're okay, I'll head back to my place now. Need to get ready for tonight's rush."

"Yes, of course, I'm fine," I shoo her away with my hand. "Just a bit dehydrated. The water helped. Thank you for being here."

"Anytime, dear. And don't forget to stop next door again soon."

"I will see you soon, I'm sure!"

She whisks out the door with her long skirt flowing behind her. It's so nice to have the place occupied again. It always seemed extra morbid to have it sit empty for so long, considering Tony was murdered right in the kitchen.

"All right, boys, time to head home."

All three of them come scurrying from the kitchen. "What did you bring us?" Marcus asks.

"What do you mean what did I bring you?"

"You're supposed to bring things back whenever you go out," Marshall explains matter of factly.

"Says who?"

"Says us. Oh, and Stumpy."

"For your information, I helped save a man's life while I was out."

"So, you didn't bring us anything?"

I groan as I turn on my heel and open the front door. I'm not sure why I bother arguing with these characters.

Chapter 15

After I get home from work, Drew texts me.

Drew: Takeout pizza for dinner tonight? My treat!

Me: Sure!

Now I'm worried - what if he knows? What if he saw me across the street from Harry's office and didn't say anything? But how could he have known, really? Maybe I'm just being paranoid.

He shows up at 6:00 PM with a veggie supreme and a bottle of pinot noir.

But just when I think I've gotten away with it. "Is there something you want to tell me?"

Uh oh. "You look extra handsome this evening. Especially carrying wine and pizza?" Okay, I tried.

"Mmmm hmmm. And?"

"All right, how did you know?"

"The door to Harry's shop just flew open at the exact right moment, and it flew open so hard the glass shattered when there wasn't even a slight breeze in the air."

He stares down at me while I gulp. "That obvious, huh?"

"Part of me is angry you were obviously hiding somewhere and watching. And yet, as much as I hate to encourage this, part of me is impressed you threw the door open with that much force."

"I was in the tea shop across the street."

"I also assume you heard the conversation."

"I did. I'm sorry you didn't get anything from it."

"We've issued an APB to all helicopter pilots in the area to be on the lookout for two men seeking transport to Gulver's Peak and the surrounding areas. If they take a job from these two then they'll be breaking the law for aiding and abetting. They're to contact law enforcement immediately if approached."

"So, you're not mad?"

"I should be mad, but you discovered the diamond smuggling theory, which is looking more and more likely." I smile. "But now I'm at a loss. No matter how many times I tell you to stay out of this, you turn right around and put yourself in the middle of everything. I'm just glad no one was hurt."

This might actually be easier if he was mad. "So now what?"

"We have to be patient and wait. Which means I keep investigating this, and we wait to hear if they contact another helicopter pilot. The good news is a helicopter is really the only way to get up to that region, so it's likely they'll try again with someone else. If and when they do, we'll get them."

I take a deep breath, "If it's any consolation, that whole situation today was pretty scary. I mean, it really hit me how close Harry was to being in danger. And how much danger you and the other agents could have been in if things went sideways. I was really shaken afterward and would prefer to avoid those kinds of close calls from now on."

"I'm glad to hear it," Drew says, looking relieved. "Now, are we going to eat or what?"

I get out plates, napkins, and wine glasses while Drew tries to talk to Stumpy. "So, he talks too, huh?" he says, looking at him while Stumpy stares back.

"He talks to the rabbits, but I can't hear him."

"But he understands you? And what happened to his back legs?"

"According to the rabbits, he does. And he told them he's a war veteran," I explain.

Drew shakes his head in disbelief. "A year ago, if someone had told me I'd be discussing actual conversations with rabbits, who happen to be decades old, and a cat who claims to be a war veteran, I'd have said they're losing it."

"And yet, here you are! Any regrets?"

I'm relieved when he says, "Nope!"

We settle down with our pizza and wine. "Your magic is getting really good. You must be practicing a lot."

I'm pleased he noticed. "I've been practicing, and Miranda has been working with me. The more confident I get, the easier and more powerful the magic is. We're going to start working on potions soon."

"If only there was a school in a faraway land you could go to, to study this," Drew laughs.

"So I could defeat the darkest wizard of all time?"

"Yes!"

"There are actual schools you can go to if you're magically inclined. Miranda went to one. My grifter parents moved around a lot, so that wasn't something I could even consider at the time. Gran would have sent me to one, but by then, I didn't want to learn magic."

"You've come a long way just in the short time you've been here."

"I'm so lucky to have met such wonderful people since I've been back. I couldn't have done it without them."

"Including your dashing boyfriend?" he teases.

"Especially my dashing boyfriend! You saved my life last year."

"Although I probably wouldn't have had to save your life if you could keep yourself away from police business."

I wave my hand in dismissal. "Details, details." Poor Drew. Eventually, he'll just give up and learn to go along with things. I'm sure of it.

Chapter 16

The next afternoon at Marcall's, I'm here alone because Damien has a dentist appointment to repair a chipped tooth. The day is winding down, and I'm thinking of closing early again when the rabbits appear at my feet.

"Hey, lady. We have something to tell you."

Oh, dear. "Okay."

"We were just out in Snowball Park eating dandelions, and that plain pancake guy was there on one of the benches talking to some other guy."

"Go on." My pulse picks up.

"We thought it might be important since that other guy was talking to you about helicopters."

They're so weird sometimes. "What other guy?"

Marcus whispers in Marshall's long ear, who then responds, "That guy who comes over to the house. The one you're always kissing."

"Detective Bailey," I sigh. Animals notice everything. Although they've been around him enough, they really don't need to refer to him as 'that guy.

"Yeah, him. He should bring us parsley, you know."

"I'll let him know, but I really need you to finish this story. What did they say?"

"We didn't hear everything because we were so busy chewing on the dandelions. Once those things go fuzzy, they're no good, so we have to get them while they're fresh."

These two can be so exasperating. "Fine! What did you hear?"

"He said something about meeting a guy from Denver at 3:00. At least, I think it was 3:00. Was it 3:00, Marshall?"

"Yeah, that sounds right."

These two are so grounded.

"Why are they meeting at 3:00?"

"We already told you."

"No, you didn't!" I shout in exasperation.

They glance at each other like I'm the most dimwitted person they know. "We said we thought it might be important because of the helicopter."

My mouth goes dry. "What about the helicopter?"

Marshall sighs loudly and rolls his eyes. "The guy from Denver is giving them a ride in a helicopter."

"Did they say where?"

They shrug at me. Never mind, I know exactly where the mobsters are going.

I'm not sure what to do next. Does Drew know about this? He must. They have an APB out. But what if this guy from Denver doesn't care? What if they offer him so much money, he decides not to turn them in? Or maybe they're forcing him to do it. Perhaps they threatened him. I have to call Drew just in case.

And, of course, he doesn't answer. The minute I get into something he thinks I shouldn't, he's around every corner. When I have an actual emergency, he's occupied.

I'll call the front desk at the station and see if they can track him down.

"Hi, Sergeant Cooper, it's Charlotte Duffin, and I'm looking for Drew."

"Hey there Charlotte, Drew's in Grand Junction this afternoon. Is there something I can help you with?"

"Grand Junction?" What? That can't be. "Why is he in Grand Junction? He didn't tell me that."

"It was a last-minute thing. He's running down a lead. Is there something I can help you with? Is this an emergency?"

What do I say now? Emergency might be stretching it. I mean it may or may not be. And what if it's all a wild goose chase? And how can I explain the rabbits were the ones who overheard the conversation? I can't just demand that he put the FBI on the phone, can I? I don't want to get Drew in trouble for sharing information with me, either.

"No, not an emergency, but if you talk to him, tell him to call me, please?"

"I will do that."

"Thanks!" I disconnect the call uneasily and pace. This may be our best chance to prove these guys want to smuggle diamonds before they drill into the mountain. But if I can't reach Drew, then what? I can't just let organized crime move into Crested Peaks.

"Boys! I'm going out. Wait for me here!"

"Don't forget the parsley!" they chorus.

I close the café and break into a run toward Harry's office. I'm hoping he's in. Better yet, I hope he's willing to help.

When I arrive, the window repairmen are there replacing the glass in his front door. I cringe. I feel bad I broke it. I'll find a way to let him know I need to pay for the damages later. Right now, we're racing against time.

"Harry!" I'm relieved to see him standing behind the counter, carefully watching the workmen.

He regards me with some caution which I understand. Considering I low key, let him believe I was here on Drew's behalf last time. He puts his hands up. "Charlotte. I've already spoken to Detective Bailey, and if I remember anything new, I'm supposed to contact him directly."

"I'm not here about that," I assure him. Well, kind of. I really need to pay for his door! "I want to hire you to fly me in your helicopter."

"Great! And when would that be?"

"Right now! It's kind of an emergency."

"Uh, well, uh, I don't normally do flights last minute. If it's an emergency, shouldn't you call the police?"

"I tried, and they weren't in."

"The police weren't in?"

Poor Harry. He looks so confused. And he keeps getting drawn into the craziness. I really won't blame him if he refuses. "Okay, Harry, I'll just be completely straight with you. I know that you're aware of everything that's going on and that you're right in the middle of it all." Harry pales. "I have it on good authority that the mob has paid a pilot from Denver to fly them to Gulver's Peak at 3:00 PM today."

He backs up as if to avoid what I'm suggesting. "You should definitely contact Detective Bailey about that."

"I did, and he's in Grand Junction for the afternoon. I'm desperate here. I think if we could just fly over the area and confirm they're there, and maybe even take some pictures, that's all we'd have to do. They might not even notice us. Just pictures, nothing more. I swear."

Harry scratches his head. "I do have a camera installed on the AStar. Companies hire me to shoot footage for commercials and tv shows and such."

I remind myself to play it cool and not jump up and down with excitement. I don't want to spook him. His previous experience with law enforcement didn't go so great after all. "That's perfect," I tell him. "Just fly right over, get some footage and leave. Turn it over to Detective Bailey, and they'll be none the wiser."

"I feel like I kind of messed up last time. I wouldn't mind making it up to the CPPD."

"You shouldn't feel bad about that at all. You did everything you could." Now I feel even worse. I don't want him thinking he's obligated to do this. Drew is right. I have a tendency to talk people into going along with my so-called schemes.

I suddenly realize that I may be more like my parents than I want to be. I just convince myself it's for the greater good and not for personal gain. "Don't put yourself at risk because of me. The police will have another shot at this some other time. Maybe we should just forget about this whole thing. I've left a message at the police station and Drew will get it sooner or later."

Just then, a helicopter flies directly over the town. It's moving fast and low and headed straight for the Gulver's Peak area. Harry and I look at each other wide-eyed. "No. You were right to begin with," Harry insists. "These are greedy criminals who think it's okay to desecrate our beautiful mountains. And then what? They infiltrate our town, and we become a hotbed of organized crime? We have to stop this before they get too far. Let's go!"

We run to the back of the building where his car is parked and then race to the helipad. I've never even been in a helicopter and have no idea what to expect. It might have been nice to take a leisurely tour first, but I guess it's too late for that now.

Harry parks next to what I assume is his AStar. I know nothing about helicopters, but I would definitely describe this as slick. It looks like the ones I've seen on television cop shows or that tv stations use for news coverage. "Wow, that's pretty nice."

Harry grins at me like a proud father. "Isn't it? Law enforcement and hospitals often use these. It maneuvers well and provides about as smooth a flight as you're going to get. That's why I like it for touring. And did you know that we have more medical helicopters than just about anywhere else because of our mountains?"

"I had no idea. It's not something I ever even thought about."

"Yep. If you're in a medical emergency in the mountains, the helicopter is your best way out."

"How did you get into all of this?" I ask as we buckle ourselves in, and he goes through his pre-flight check.

"Marine Corps," he offers simply.

I nod my head and sigh in relief. We're in good hands.

Next thing I know we're in the air and flying toward Gulver's Peak. The view from up here is stunning and I remind myself to take a tour for fun when this is all over. I wonder if Drew has ever done this? Assuming he's still speaking to me after this, I could take him on a romantic date in a helicopter.

I don't realize how tightly I'm gripping the door handle until Harry reminds me to breathe. I'm not that scared. But this is quite the experience. Damien and Miranda won't know what to think when they hear about all of this.

As we skim effortlessly over the treetops, I'm stunned by how breathtaking the scenery is. If I thought it was majestic to stand at the bottom of the mountains and look up, it's a whole other world to see it up here. I'm almost in tears at how beautiful it is. Then I'm angry over the thought of criminals drilling into the mountain for diamonds.

"Look over there," Harry's voice comes through the headset. There's a glint in the distance as something reflects the sunlight. As we get closer, we see it's the same helicopter that flew over us in town a little while ago. "Got em! I want to make sure I get clear footage of the tail number."

He flies a little closer than I'd like, but I guess if we've come this far, there's no sense in only doing it halfway. We see three men walking around below us, and when they look straight up at us, I get a bad feeling. "Uh, Harry, I think we have enough. We should get back now."

"I agree. Let's go home."

Harry banks sharply in the direction we came from and heads back to the helipad. "We did it, kid!" he shouts as we fist bump. As impressive as this whole trip was, I'll be glad to have my feet on solid ground again. I'm also hoping it will soften the blow for Drew when he sees the footage we got.

While looking out the side window though, I catch a glimpse of something in my peripheral vision, and I turn in my seat as a chill runs through me. "Uhhhh, Harry."

"I see em'," he grunts.

I'm not sure if they're following us or chasing us but either way, I don't like it. "What do we do now?"

"Leave it to me."

I grip the seat tightly as Harry makes moves I'm not even sure how to describe. He races this way and that while sweat coats my forehead. Thankfully I notice the more nervous I get, the calmer he seems to get.

"What are they doing?" I squeak.

"They're just trying to intimidate us," Harry explains.

"I think they're doing an outstanding job at it."

"Nah, we'll be okay," Harry says as he deftly maneuvers through a patch of clouds.

"What if they shoot at us?"

"If they were going to shoot at us, they would have done it already. They're just hoping I'll get nervous and do something stupid. But they don't know who they're dealing with," he turns to grin at me. "Like riding a bike," he proclaims, banking sharply to the left again.

I notice the other pilot has trouble keeping up with us, but that doesn't make me feel a whole lot better. I know I keep telling Drew that I've had enough and that I'll stay out of police work this time for sure. But this time for sure, for sure, is it. I swear. I never intended to get us involved in a duel in the clouds.

And while I wouldn't dare use any of my unpracticed witchcraft on a helicopter, I've already engaged the spell that ensures I don't get motion sick during this wild ride. The first time I read about it in one of Miranda's spell books I thought it was silly.

But now I'm glad I memorized it. It's a spell I can only use on myself, but it works to stabilize my inner ear and trick it into thinking I'm just standing perfectly still on the ground. Harry obviously doesn't need it. His focus is razor-sharp and unphased.

When I hear a siren, I'm sure I'm imagining it. What could be making that kind of noise clear up here? I still turn around in my seat to look. "Harry!" I shriek. "There's another one!" That's it. We are truly dead up here. We're being chased by not one but two mafia helicopters, and we don't stand a chance.

"Hello boys, just in time!" Harry exclaims.

What is he talking about? He's acting like they're friends of his or something. "It's the FBI," he explains when he sees my stricken look. "Some helicopters have sirens."

"Oh!" Is all I can manage.

Soon, the helicopter from Denver streaks past us, the FBI hot on its tail.

"Should we follow them?" Harry asks.

"No!" I shriek.

He laughs. "I was just kidding; we really are going home now."

"Oh, I knew that."

He laughs again. Yeah, this is just hilarious.

When we arrive at the helipad, there are cop cars and FBI everywhere. Oh boy. I think I've really done it this time. I wonder if it's too much to hope for that maybe Drew is still in Grand Junction and missed this entire thing? But as we land, I see him leaning against his car, his arms crossed over his chest and looking none too pleased. Yeah, I could have guessed that.

The moment the helicopter blades stop, we're swarmed with just about every type of law enforcement personnel we can imagine. They don't have guns drawn or anything, so I'm hoping we aren't in too much trouble. I turn to Harry, "I'm so sorry I got you into this. I have a bad habit of doing things like this."

Harry looks at me strangely. "Are you kidding? That's the most fun I've had in quite a while. Having to talk to those guys face to face just left me speechless and out of control. But this..." He pats the control panel. "This is where I thrive. I could have said no to you after all."

"So, we're good?" I ask.

"We are more than good. Thank you for that."

Harry seems to have a strange sense of thankfulness, but I'll take it. As for me. I've never been happier to put my feet on solid ground.

"Ms. Duffin, you'll need to come with us, please," one of the FBI agents announces.

We walk towards Drew when he says, "I can take it from here, guys, thanks."

"Sure thing, Detective."

The agents slowly fade away as Drew and I come face to face. "Are you okay?" he asks.

"My knees are a little wobbly, but considering everything else, yes, I'm good. Thanks to Harry."

"The FBI just forced the helicopter down in Gunnison, and they're taking both men into custody as we speak."

"Both?" I'm confused. "There should have been three men."

"It was just the helicopter pilot and the geologist."

"What? What about The Jackal?"

Drew gives me that look, "We still don't know if that guy is The Jackal."

"How can he not be?"

"Charlotte."

"All right, fine. But whoever he is, he got away?"

"It looks like it."

"So there goes the whole case?"

"The FBI is interrogating both men right now. Hopefully, they'll give everybody up and let us know where the other guy is, and it will all be over soon."

"What about Harry?" I ask as I glance back to see him being put into the back of a police car.

"He's fine. He's not under arrest. They just need to get his official statement, and he'll be free to go."

"Why were you in Grand Junction?" I ask, suddenly remembering how all of this started.

Drew sighs and runs his hand over his short hair. "We were sent there on a wild goose chase. Considering what just went down, the mafia obviously wanted us distracted, so they could get in there without interruption and determine what their next move would be.

"Hopefully, at least the geologist turns on his partners, so we can determine what their exact plans are for getting diamonds out of the mountain and then out of Colorado."

"Bet they didn't count on the meddling girlfriend."

Drew cracks just the slightest smile, and I swear it's the hottest thing I've ever seen. He nods his head. "They didn't count on the meddling girlfriend."

"We only intended to get camera footage of them in that spot. We weren't there to chase them down or anything like that. Just pictures. Then straight home. We just hadn't anticipated a chase."

"You can tell all of that to the FBI in your statement."

"Am I under arrest?"

"No, of course not. You just need to give a statement like Harry is doing." At that, he signals to an FBI agent who comes to get me.

"I have a lot of paperwork to finish myself, and we're still waiting to learn the outcome of the interrogation in Gunnison, but let me know as soon as the FBI releases you, okay?"

"I will," I tell him, nodding in relief that he doesn't seem that mad for once.

Chapter 17

After I give my statement to the FBI, Drew drives me back to Marcall's to get the rabbits and Stumpy. Then he takes me home. "Both the helicopter pilot and Dr Natt are still being questioned, but so far it looks like they don't know much about who is doing what within the organization."

"Surely, they're just lying to save themselves, right?" I ask. After all this, they can't just get away with it.

"I don't think so," Drew explains. "We're offering them a heck of a deal to roll over on any of these guys they've been working with, but they're still very vague on names and places. Sounds like the mob told them just enough to get them on board with the diamond smuggling operation but not much more than that."

"So it is diamond smuggling for sure?"

"Indeed. You were dead on with that all along."

"Hmmm, not so bad for a meddling girlfriend mediocre witch, huh?"

"You are far more than a mediocre witch Char. Although meddling girlfriend might be pretty accurate."

Even I have to agree with him on the last part. "But what about The Jackal? Where is he?"

"If you mean Creepy Stranger, we don't know. He's in the wind. As soon as the three of them saw you guys, they say he took off and sprinted straight into the trees. They obviously couldn't wait for him, so they took off in the helicopter. We have agents scouring that area right now but so far, nothing."

"But what did the two you have in custody say about him?"

"Very little. The mafia is highly secretive when it comes to their operatives. Unless you've been with them for a while, they don't share information about their inner circle."

"That's ridiculous. He's The Jackal. I just know it!"

Drew shakes his head. "I hope we can find him and bring him in. Only then will we know for sure."

"But what if you don't find him? Then what?"

"The diamond smuggling shouldn't be an issue anymore. If any of them were to even think about making another move on the area, we'll know. We've effectively shut that part of the operation down."

"So that's it? That's all there is? Kind of anti-climactic, isn't it?"

"Welcome to police work. Not every case is wrapped up neatly and tied with a pretty bow at the end. Although I'm not sure how a helicopter chase is anti-climactic," Drew says, turning to me as we pull up in front of my house.

"I really wanted to catch The Jackal, though."

"So do I, but you have to remember there's a reason that the FBI has been after this guy forever and still haven't caught him. He's incredibly clever. We may never catch him."

"What? That's horrible!"

"I know, but unfortunately, we don't always catch the bad guys. And we have to be okay with that, or it will eat us alive."

The more I think about it, the more I realize I appreciate just being a simple witch and vegetarian breakfast café owner.

Chapter 18

After about a week, the town is finally quieting down again. Being swarmed by the FBI was a bit maddening. And it was all over the national news. But now that it's over, and we all feel safe again, I keep telling myself that maybe it will be a nice benefit to the local businesses at least.

Surely, the tourists don't think we're overrun with crime. I watched some of the coverage on the news, and there was a lot of footage of snow-capped mountain peaks combined with the colorful spring flowers.

I'm pleasantly surprised when Rita, my landlord, walks into Marcall's this morning. "Rita! How nice to see you! It's been a minute."

"That's what happens when you leave the country for three months," she says, laughing.

"Leave the country?"

"Yes, silly, I've been in South America all winter, and I just arrived in Crested Peaks this morning. Although I see you had some more excitement here recently."

Rita owns the building that Marcall's, Alice's Tavern, and several other shops and restaurants lease on this side of the street. She inherited it after her husband, who was almost her ex-husband at the time, was murdered by a guy he tried to double-cross in a land deal. They planned to tear down all of the shops to build high-rise condos.

I was relieved that when all the dust settled, that she decided to keep the shops and continue renting them to the current tenants. Except, of course, Tony next door, who was also killed in the mayhem.

"I didn't even realize that you were out of the country. I just thought I hadn't seen you around because of the freezing cold winter."

Rita smiles, "Thanks to my spectacular assistant, who kept everything running so smoothly, it sounds like most people didn't even realize I wasn't here. By the way, what do you think of Alice?" she gestures with her head to indicate my new neighbor.

"Oh, she's great. She's doing a ton of business over there!"

"I'm eager to meet her."

"You haven't met her yet?"

"Well, no silly, how could I meet her when I'm out of the country? My assistant has handled everything with the rental. It's like she just appeared from out of nowhere. I was sure she'd insist on an even bigger discount than I was already offering – given what happened there last year.

"You know I had a heck of a time renting that place out. But she didn't even haggle, just said she'd take the place and wanted to move in immediately. I was thrilled. I'm even more thrilled to hear the place is doing well."

Now I'm confused. I'm certain that when I first met Alice, she mentioned how Rita told her I was a witch. She also mentioned that even though Rita drove a hard bargain, she negotiated a great deal on the rent.

"But you were at the grand opening just the other day," I protest.

"Honey, do you need your hearing checked? I just told you that I just got back to town this morning."

"But you obviously talked to her on the phone, right?"

"Nope! Not a word. It was all so easy that by the time my assistant let me know she had a potential tenant, Alice had already signed on the dotted line."

What on earth is going on here? "Oh. Well, I'm glad that it all worked out for you!"

"Me too! Sorry to cut our reunion short, but I'm going to head over there right now and see if I can catch her. It was great to see you again, and I'm glad business is obviously going well for you too. Let's grab lunch sometime next week and catch up!"

"Yes, let's do that!" I tell her.

I'm not sure why this makes me so uneasy, but it all just seems rather odd. The first time I met Alice, and she brought up my being a witch, I was concerned that she had an issue with it. But when she said Rita told her, I decided she was just making conversation.

And talking to Rita just now triggered something else. Alice had said something about meeting my handsome police officer boyfriend when I know for a fact, I hadn't said anything about that beforehand. Yet somehow, she just knew.

And if Rita hadn't told her any of this, then who did? I have no idea who Rita's assistant is, so I don't think it was her. The unease grows as it settles around me like a thick cloud. I also think about how weird it seemed when Alice got the work permits in record time and then completely moved into the restaurant in the middle of the night.

I consider calling Drew, but what am I supposed to tell him? He's extra happy these days that my diamond smuggling theory panned out. But I'm not sure how thrilled he'd be to hear me say Alice is kind of creeping me out.

Then I ponder discussing it with Damien, but after the helicopter chase he's even more skittish than ever about me "sticking my nose where it doesn't belong" as he likes to say. I swear he almost vomited. When I told him the whole story he was really upset. I know he's worried I'm going to eventually do something that will get me killed.

For the rest of the afternoon, I tell myself that Alice is probably just one of those people who wants to be in everybody's business. Some people are like that. Personally, I think it's a little creepy but whatever.

After we close and Damien leaves, on a hunch, I decide to visit Harvey. It's a nice day, and I promised him I'd stop by and see him after all. Just to say hello. Except on my way out the door, I grab one of the flyers from Alice's Tavern. It couldn't hurt to ask.

I walk down to the hotel, and wouldn't you know it, Harvey is out front greeting guests. Most already seem to know about the ghosts, but some are quite startled to see a 19th century ghost tipping his hat and welcoming them to the hotel.

"Good afternoon, Harvey!"

"Charlotte! How nice to see you. Did you stop by just to say hello?"

"I promised you I would!" I feel kind of guilty. I'm not lying exactly. I did promise him I would. It's just not today. But I'm willing to chat with him for a while if it makes him feel better. I realize I'll owe more than one person in this town once this is all over. Who knew you had to lie so much when investigating crimes?

After all, I still don't know where any of this will lead me. Naturally, we talk about what went down with the diamond smuggling sting. I remind Harvey that he played a big role in that because of his watchful eye, and he puffs up with pride. It's true, after all. And yes, I'm buttering him up, hoping he won't notice when I ask him a question. "Hey Harvey, quick question."

"Yes, dear."

I pull the flyer from my pocket and unfold it carefully. "Have you ever seen this woman by any chance?"

"Why yes, as a matter of fact, I saw her several times with the first man that was killed. Why do you ask? Did they arrest her too?"

"Uh no, I was just wondering. I should probably be getting back to Marcall's now anyway. Don't want to leave Damien there alone for too long."

"Thanks for stopping by. You'll come back soon, yes?"

"I promise!" And this time, I mean it. But now I have to hightail it back to the café. My heart races as goosebumps line my arms, and I try to decide what to do next. I don't know how Alice is involved in all of this, but she has to be.

Too many things about her seem weirdly coincidental, but I don't really believe in coincidence. Especially not here and especially now that I realize she knew Bubblegum Vinny.

I try calling Drew, but of course, he doesn't pick up. "Really?!" I shout out loud at the phone before the voicemail kicks in. "Hey Drew, I just talked to Harvey at the hotel, and he gave me some very disturbing news that you need to hear. Call me or come by Marcall's when you get this."

I arrive back at the café and try to decide my next move. If only I would hear from Drew soon. What does this all mean? Is Alice part of the mob? That sounds crazy, and yet it doesn't.

But what about Creepy Stranger, who hasn't been seen since Gulver's Peak? Did Alice kill him and dump his body somewhere? Was I right to begin with, and he's The Jackal and took off when the FBI arrested everyone?

"What's wrong, lady?" Marshall asks when he sees me pacing. "You look troubled."

"This is going to sound weird, but I need to decide what to do about Alice."

"Good news! You don't have to do anything about Alice."

"Why is that?"

"We heard her say she was leaving town for a while."

"Oh no, are you sure?"

"Yes," Marcus adds. "She said she had to return to Chicago to deal with business there."

These animals overhear everything!

"When did she say that?"

"I think it was a couple of hours ago," Marcus tells me, looking at his brother for confirmation.

"Oh, it was definitely a couple of hours ago. Although we don't tell time very well so it may have been longer. Or shorter. We're not sure."

Great. So helpful and yet not so helpful.

I have to stop her from leaving if I'm not already too late. I'll just have to hope that Drew stops by here instead of calling. And soon!

"If Drew comes by, tell him..." The rabbits look at me with blank faces. Drew can't communicate with them. "Never mind."

I hurry over to Alice's Tavern, and thankfully, the door is unlocked. I burst through it breathlessly, and Alice is at the bar signing some paperwork. Her suitcases are on the floor next to her. Thank goodness!

"Alice!" I shout, startling her so badly she nearly jumps straight out of her seat.

"Charlotte!" she responds with her hand to her chest. "You nearly frightened me to death. Is everything okay?"

"Oh. Yes. I'm sorry. I didn't mean to startle you."

"What's so urgent?"

Great. I raced over here with no plan whatsoever.

"I, uh, well, uh, I just wanted to say hello. And tell you to have a good trip." I point at her suitcases.

"Oh, thank you, I appreciate that. I'm not sure how long I'll have to be gone. How did you know I was leaving?"

Oh, these darn rabbits. They may overhear helpful information, but how am I supposed to admit that? "I didn't know that until I saw your suitcases. And then I assumed you were going out of town."

"But you said you came by to tell me to have a good trip. How could you have known that?"

I'm sweating like crazy. If only I could use witchcraft to help me come up with a better story. And now Alice is really looking at me suspiciously.

"I came by to say hello, and then I saw your suitcases and decided it would be polite to tell you to have a good trip," I'm cringing, just listening to myself.

"You came bursting through the door like it was a matter of life or death, it hardly seems like you stopped by just to say hello."

My mind is whirling, and I can't think of a single plausible thing to say. "Nothing is wrong back in Chicago, is it? I mean, I hope everything is all right."

"Just some business with the restaurant back there that needs my attention, that's all. Why are you so sweaty and flushed? You're acting strangely."

"I was just out walking, and it's pretty warm out."

"Okay, well, glad you're all right. I need to be heading out now, though, so I'm going to lock up and—"

"No!" I shout so abruptly she nearly jumps again as I throw myself in her path. Where is Drew?

"Charlotte, if I didn't know any better, I'd say you're trying to prevent me from leaving."

"Now why, would I do that?" I tell, her trying to laugh in a way that makes the very idea sound preposterous, but it comes out sounding really fake.

"You tell me," she says as she puts one hand on her hip and looks at me crossly. I can tell she's losing patience fast and getting increasingly suspicious of me. "I think you know more than you're letting on." She's no longer the extremely friendly eccentric older lady from next door. Her face has taken on a harsh form, and I regret coming over here by myself. "Jake!" she shouts suddenly.

Jake? Who's Jake? I gasp out loud when Creepy Stranger walks out of her kitchen. I am in deep, deep trouble. "You!" I blurt out and instantly regret it.

Alice shakes her head, "Just as I suspected."

My mind races. I can crack her across the head with a levitating liquor bottle from the bar, which could be enough distraction for me to run at least. But I'm not skilled enough to send two bottles in opposite directions to render Jake unconscious as well. Why haven't I practiced more?

"Don't even think about it," she growls like she's reading my mind. She snaps her fingers at Jake, and he pulls out a gun from his waistband and points it at me.

I can't believe this is happening again. I've got to keep stalling somehow.

"I knew you were The Jackal," I scowl at him.

"Ha!" Alice shouts, startling us both. I turn to her. "I have worked nearly all my life to build up this empire. Me! A mere woman!"

Um. What?

She thumps her hand against her chest. "I'm the smart one! I'm the tough one! I'm the clever one! And yet everybody assumes The Jackal just has to be a man!"

I stare at her wide eyed and in shock.

"Yes, that's right, I'm The Jackal! I'm the mastermind behind this entire thing. And I have been for nearly 30 years! I've been unstoppable. At first, I thought it was cute that no one seemed to know who I was.

"I built my reputation on it. I enjoyed all the power I secretly amassed, but I'm not getting any younger, and dangit, I want some credit! Why can't a woman be the head of one of the most powerful crime factions in the country? Why?"

Does she really expect an answer, or is this just a rhetorical question? And why am I even wondering about that when I have a gun pointed at me? And I'm standing in front of one of the FBI's most wanted criminals of all time.

"Did you kill Bubblegum Vinny?" I ask. If I'm going to die anyway, I might as well get some answers.

"Of course, I killed him! Do you think anything takes place on my turf without my say so? He turned snitch. Said he wanted to retire and was going to turn himself into the FBI. I couldn't have that, so I shot him."

Jake smiles back at her. What a creep. I knew it all along.

"What infuriates me is that my entire diamond smuggling plan was thwarted by some two-bit mountain cop—"

"—hey now…" I interrupt.

She stares daggers at me, "—and his dimwitted girlfriend."

"I'm obviously not that dimwitted if I helped stop you, am I?"

She steps toward me. "Do you really think you're in any position to make wisecracks at me?"

She looks over at Jake, "Just shoot her."

"Wait!" I shout as I wave my hands in the air. I know I need to concentrate harder than I've ever concentrated in my entire life if I hope to stop any bullets that he fires at me, and I'm not sure I can do that. Especially with my heart racing and my mind whirling. And I might be able to stop one, but there's no way I could stop more than one at a time.

"Stop stalling! Shoot her now!"

"You really want me to shoot her here? It will leave such a mess. Let me just take her somewhere that no one will find the body. She'll disappear without a trace," Jake argues.

"What do I care about a mess? I'm leaving," she retorts.

"If they find a bloody mess here and you've disappeared, you'll be their number one suspect. If I take her somewhere else and kill her, they'll just decide you left and won't think much of it."

Alice, I mean The Jackal, ponders his argument for a moment, "Nope. Still don't care. And if you don't shoot her, I will." With that, she reaches behind the bar and pulls out a gun to point at me too.

Great. Now I have two people who want to shoot me. There is absolutely no way I can stop bullets from two different guns at once. I'm dead.

"If you want something done right, you have to do it yourself," she smiles the evilest smile I've ever witnessed when Jake suddenly says.

"I can't allow you to do that." Then he turns the gun on her.

What?! Now I'm really confused. What is happening here?

"What the hell?" Alice responds. Clearly unsure as to which way to point her own gun now.

"Drop the gun Alice," he demands. I can't take my eyes off either of them; I'm so confused. Part of me is shouting inside my head run while they're distracted except, I'm distracted myself. What is Creepy Stranger, I mean Jake, doing?

"I'm with the FBI."

"No, you're not!" Alice laughs.

"I'm undercover. I've been deep undercover with your organization for three years."

Alice looks momentarily stunned. She obviously can't believe this all happened on her watch. Ha! Not so clever after all, huh Alice?

Then she turns the gun on Jake. Who suddenly isn't so creepy. Or a stranger. While they're pointing their guns at each other my brain is telling me to run but my feet are stuck to the floor. It's like I'm mesmerized by watching these two stare each other down. I can't let her shoot him. He saved my life. Why doesn't he just shoot her?

And then it happens. A blazing hot energy builds inside of me, and somehow, I know she's going to fire first. I don't know how I know this; I just feel it all the way to my toes. Why doesn't he just shoot her?

The voice in my head screams at me, do something! I concentrate on the nearest bottle of liquor sitting on the bar and fling it at her gun. I hit it, but It's too late. She fires anyway, and I watch in horror as Jake falls to the ground.

She whirls toward me and fires again just in time for me to unstick my feet from the floor and dive under a table. She continues firing as I scramble to get away. My heart races so fast I'm convinced it might explode at any second.

I claw at the wood floor as I struggle to keep my head down and find the next barrier to duck behind. I finally remember to focus on her bullets when I can and even manage to knock one of them astray.

I know I can only keep this up for so long, though. How many freakin bullets does she have? And then it happens. I run out of tables to duck behind, and now we're face to face. My efforts to catch my breath sound unnaturally loud as it echoes throughout the bar.

Alice's calm demeanor is chilling as she stares at me with such malice preparing to fire one last time. I catch a glimpse of a chair behind her and send all of my energy to it. I slide it straight to the back of her legs, where it hits her exactly at knee level, and she plops down in it as if she meant to sit in that chair all along.

The look of surprise on her face would almost be laughable if she didn't still have a gun in her hand. But when she points the gun at me again, shattering glass and splintering wood rain down on top of us as I cover my head and think that the sky must be falling for sure.

The FBI and the Crested Peaks Police Department seem to be flying in the tavern from every direction. They're all shouting at her to drop her gun and get down on the floor. Meanwhile, I'm hunched over with my hands covering my ears and shaking like a leaf.

It feels like an earthquake. There are so many of them. One of them throws Alice to the ground as her gun skitters away and they leap on top of her to subdue her.

"Jake!" I yell, pointing at his lifeless body that's surrounded by a pool of blood. "Jake was shot!"

Several officers run to help him, as I hear. "Charlotte! Charlotte! Where are you?" It's Drew!

"Drew!" I call out as he leaps over overturned chairs and tables to get to me, broken glass crunching under his feet. He clutches at my arms while pulling me up. He checks me everywhere. "Are you okay? Are you hurt? Are you bleeding?"

"I'm all right," I reassure him. Sure, I have a few bruises from repeatedly diving to the ground, plus I'm sure there's little pieces of glass and wood tangled in my hair, but otherwise, I'm in one piece. "But Jake, he got shot! I tried to stop her, but I was too late."

"It's okay; they'll take care of him. I just need to know you're okay."

"I think so, yeah. And I am really glad to see you!" I tell him, nearly bursting into tears as I throw my arms around him and squeeze him as tight as I can.

"I got your message and went straight to the café. Those crazy rabbits and that cat wouldn't let up. I knew something was wrong when I found the door open, and you weren't there, but the three of them kept pulling on my pants and butting their heads into my legs. It sounds ludicrous, but somehow I knew they were pushing me in the direction of the tavern."

"I'm going to owe them extra parsley now." I sigh. "And some catnip for Stumpy."

Chapter 19

"A little to the right. No, wait, now a little to the left. Okay, back to the right again. Wait…"

"Oh, just stop it!" I scold Marcus, who is obviously just messing with me now. The rabbits run off giggling, with Stumpy right behind them.

I'm trying to decorate the café for the Easter festivities this weekend. On Saturday we're hosting a huge party. Damien is the one who thought of it. He felt like we needed a celebration after what happened at Alice's Tavern and to welcome spring in a better way than a mafia shootout.

After the chaos that went on there and considering the amount of time it will take Rita to clean and repair everything, unfortunately leaving the place vacant once again, I agreed with Damien. We're hosting a massive brunch with a menu featuring the most amazing garden vegetable tamales you can imagine, courtesy of Damien.

And of course, no Marcall's event would be complete without his mouth-watering black beans. We haven't forgotten the traditional brunch goodies either: potatoes, pancakes, eggs, fruit, hot cross buns (which the rabbits weren't so sure about until I told them it refers to rolls), and plenty of mimosas.

The whole town is buzzing about the party. We'll close off the street in order to put plenty of tables and chairs out front since Marcall's isn't big enough to accommodate an entire town all at once. The best part is, Rita is paying for the entire thing. She's hoping it will bring about some good juju since she hasn't had great luck recently.

Once the repairs are complete, she's insisting that any potential tenants will be fully vetted by her personally. Not that she blames her assistant for what happened. Who could have imagined one of the most notorious mafioso of all time would take up residence in our sleepy mountain town?

As I rearrange the decorative lights one more time, this time without the rabbits' help, I'm delighted to see Jake walk in the door. Yes, his first name really is Jake. He explained that when undercover, it's easier to keep his first name the same. Fewer lies to forget that way.

He looks fabulous. Although considering he was lying on the floor of the tavern, pale and lifeless just a short time ago, almost anything where he's upright would look better.

"I heard someone is having a party!" he says, beaming at us, his arm bound up in a sling.

"And you're the first to arrive!" I consider hugging him, but I don't want to hurt his shoulder.

It turns out that my hitting Alice in the head with the liquor bottle actually saved Jake's life because instead of shooting him center mass like she intended, she ended up shooting him in the shoulder instead. After surgery and some physical therapy, he should be okay.

"Please, sit down! Have a mimosa! Early!" I laugh.

"I can only stay for a bit; I have a flight to Miami I have to catch, but I wanted to thank you again for saving my life, and I brought you this."

He holds up the Guide to Colorado Gemstones book I saw in his briefcase. My mouth drops open in embarrassment. I'd forgotten all about the book I saw him with. "Drew mentioned that you saw this in my briefcase and were convinced that I had stolen it from the library."

"I am so embarrassed," I stammer. "I don't know what to say." When he laughs, I'm even more embarrassed. I admit it, sometimes my imagination gets way out of control.

"I wanted you to know that I didn't steal it from the library. I bought it at the local bookstore as part of my undercover work."

"Of course, you did."

"But now I would like you to keep it. To remember me by." He laughs again, and I'm glad that he finds this amusing because I just feel like a dope. I'm glad he isn't mad about it, at least.

"I will keep it forever. It will be a good reminder that I need to be much more careful before jumping to conclusions about people."

"You mean people who eat plain pancakes or just the next time you investigate a crime?" he asks with a twinkle still in his eye. Drew talks way too much.

"No! I am done with crime investigation." I hold my hand in the air like I'm swearing an oath. Although I'm pretty sure I've done this before. But this time, I really swear. "I'm leaving that to the professionals from now on. I'm just a café owner and happy to be one at that."

Then I hold my left hand out to shake his, considering his right hand is bound up in the sling. "And you are welcome back here any time for more pancakes. Plain or otherwise."

He smiles and shakes my hand. "Don't sell yourself short. You helped uncover a major diamond smuggling operation, after all. And unmasked The Jackal."

"Don't tell Drew that! I'm already in enough trouble as it is."

"Oh, I'm sure he'll get over it eventually. And he's just worried about you."

Once Drew realized I was okay and that Jake would be okay, I got the longest lecture ever on why I needed to stop my amateur investigating. He had to point out that even though I've only been back in Crested Peaks for a short time, I've already been held at gunpoint by criminals twice.

And under two entirely different circumstances. But I maintain that I don't go looking for these things on purpose. They just find me.

Drew's ears must be burning because he shows up shortly after Jake leaves for the airport. "I see you got the book. The book that was not stolen from the library."

"I did, and Jake seems to think it was funny."

"Oh, it was hilarious all right," Drew responds, rolling his eyes at me. "Now, where are the mimosas?"

"First, I need your help in the back. Damien ordered a pile of rabbit-themed tablecloths, and I need your big muscles to help me carry them up here."

Drew tilts his head at me. "Huh. Considering I know you can just magic them up here by yourself, I'm guessing you're just trying to flatter me and my big muscles."

"Whatever. Just help me."

Drew dutifully follows me into the back room as I show him the tablecloths. They're covered in colorful rabbits in a variety of poses. Sitting, hopping, and sleeping. I hold one up for him to check out while the rabbits stare at it in disdain. "That's not what real rabbits look like," Marshall informs me.

"They just for decoration," I point out while both rabbits stomp their feet with displeasure.

I nearly drop an entire box of them when Damien bursts through the kitchen door with a wild look on his face.

"What now?" Drew asks like he's afraid to even know.

"Code Red!" he hisses at me.

"No way!" I hiss back.

"Yes way! Code Red!"

Drew looks at both of us like we've finally lost our marbles while I shove the box of tablecloths into his arms.

Damien and I race to the kitchen door, then stop and compose ourselves before heading back into the dining area. After I saw the reality tv star in the grocery store, but didn't tell Damien about it right away, we pinky swore that the next time anything like that happened, the person who did the spotting would declare a Code Red. Meanwhile the other person had to drop everything and come running. I didn't realize we'd get to use it so soon.

We leave the kitchen like it was the most normal thing in the world, and there they are. The guy I saw in the grocery store and the 4th place finisher. Not the one the world thinks he's engaged to. Damien and I stare at them with our mouths hanging open. We can't think of a thing to say.

Thankfully, Drew finally pushes past us to greet our latest visitors. "Welcome to Marcall's! Can I get something started for you?"

"We just wondered what all the fuss was about, so we decided to stop in and ask. I hope it's okay?" the guy from the grocery store says as he looks at us like he's worried something is seriously wrong with us.

"We're having an Easter Spring celebration tomorrow, and the entire town is invited, and we'd love to see you there!" Drew explains.

"That sounds like fun. We'd love to come!" the woman, whose name has completely flown out of my brain from shock, replies.

Meanwhile, Damien and I still stand there like Ralph meeting Santa Claus at the mall. Incapable of forming words that make a bit of sense. I think by the time they're walking out the door, he manages something like "bleep bleep bloop."

Drew turns to the two of us after the door closes. "You can successfully fend off armed criminals, but a couple of reality tv stars show up unexpectedly, and you can't speak?"

"What just happened?" Damien asks.

"I don't know," I mumble, still dumbstruck from the whole thing.

Later, when Miranda and Miles join our pre-party party, and Miles sees me holding the book he says, "Hey, I didn't get the chance to tell you that I found the library's copy of that book under one of the bean bags in the reading nook.

"Someone must have been looking through it and didn't put it away like they're supposed to. I can't stand it when they do that. It's not that hard just to put it back on one of the re-shelving carts."

Miranda, Damien, and I look at each other and laugh. I'd say we'd had too many mimosas, but we're really just getting started.

Thank You!

Thank you for reading 24 Carrot Caper

Sign up for my email list here: https://mailchi.mp/9ebce0da866a-/email-signup-list

Visit my website biskinnerauthor.com

Follow me on Instagram @bethiskinner Facebook @biskinner-author TikTok @biskinner

9 798201 520243